Footprints In The

Snow

VIVIAN SINCLAIR

Copyright

This book is a work of fiction. Names, characters, places, and incidents are the product of the author's imagination or are used fictitiously. Any resemblance to actual events, locales, or persons, living or dead, is entirely coincidental.

Published by East Hill Books

Cover design: Vivian Sinclair Books

Cover illustrations credit:
© Mikaelmales | Dreamstime.com

ISBN-13: 978-1537758787
ISBN-10: 1537758780

To find out about new releases and about other books written by Vivian Sinclair visit her website at VivianSinclairBooks.com or follow her on the Author page at Amazon or on GoodReads.com

Virginia Lovers Trilogy - contemporary romance:

    Book 1 – Alexandra's Garden

    Book 2 – Ariel's Summer Vacation

    Book 3 – Lulu's Christmas Wish

A Guest At The Ranch – western contemporary romance

Maitland Legacy, A Family Saga Trilogy - western contemporary romances

    Book 1, Lost In Wyoming – Lance's story

    Book 2, Moon Over Laramie – Tristan's story

    Book 3, Christmas In Cheyenne – Raul's story

Wyoming Christmas Trilogy – western contemporary romances

    Book 1 – Footprints In The Snow – Tom's story

    Book 2 – A Visitor For Christmas – Brianna's story

Book 3 – Trapped On The Mountain – Chris' story

Seattle Rain series - women's fiction novels

Book 1 - A Walk In The Rain

Book 2 – Rain, Again!

Book 3 – After The Rain

Storm In A Glass Of Water, a small town story

PROLOGUE

Laramie, Wyoming, Two years earlier

There were only a few days left until Christmas and Tom was satisfied that after attending some business meetings in town, he bought gifts for his family. The sky turned dark and scattered flurries came from the clouds. It would not be long before they changed into real snowfall. Tom hoped to be back home on the ranch by then.

He had only one more item on his list. His sister Brianna heard of this newly opened Thai restaurant in Laramie. Tom was a true rancher. Meat and potatoes were his food of choice, and plenty of it, after a day of hard work on the range. However, Brianna liked to try new, fancy things of all sorts, not only food. Who knew from what ancestor she got this fancy taste.

So here was Tom, on a cold afternoon, instead of driving home before the snow covered the roads entirely, looking for the new Thai restaurant. Ah, here it was! 'Wild Lotus'. Tom wrinkled his nose. How could a lotus be wild? An unbroken horse, or an unruly bull, now that was wild, but a lotus flower....

He opened the door to enter when he bumped into a tall woman who was exiting just then, followed by her much shorter friend. He stepped back to let them pass.

"Ladies," he said politely inclining his head. The taller one looked at him with familiar blue-green eyes. His mouth opened in surprise, "Oh!"

Faith Parker stopped and smiled at him. "Tom, how are you?" And because the second woman had stopped near her and was looking from her to Tom with undisguised curiosity, she added, "You know Lottie, don't you?"

"I was Charlotte Evans in high school," the short one piped in.

Tom didn't remember any Charlotte Evans from high school, but even if he did, his mind was scrambled and in shock at seeing again the woman he had adored for most of his life and who left him a year and a half ago. "Ah, yes of course," he answered only because they expected it of him. He looked at Faith. She was beautiful and radiant. It seemed her marriage to Raul Maitland made her happy. Ah, right, the marriage. "Congrats on your recent marriage, Faith," he replied politely like talking about the weather, and not like his heart was breaking.

"Thank you, Tom," she said, her smile widening, lighting up her whole face. "Your turn will come soon. A lucky lady will get you to the altar," she joked, forgetting that he had asked her to marry him three times, and she had rejected him every time.

Now, how to answer this hare-brained idea? "Yes, well, we'll see," he muttered. "If you'll excuse me..." And with this, he made his escape, entering the restaurant.

He took a seat, breathed deeply, counted to ten, and then he tried to remember where he was and for what purpose.

Tom Gorman had been a happy fellow. It was not easy to live and make a living on a cattle ranch in the harsh climate of southeastern Wyoming. Yet Tom couldn't imagine life anywhere else but here, on the land settled by his ancestors, land that belonged to his family for a century and a half. Here he was happy. In the wide spaces of Wyoming, he was at home and hard work even in the dead of winter didn't scare him.

When his father died and he had to step in and take care of the ranch, his carefree days were gone. He had always been hard-working, but the major decisions were made by his father. Now he had no one to rely on but himself. Slowly his happy-go-lucky nature gave way to a more serious manner. That changed into a downright somber one, when his intended, the beautiful Faith Parker, told him she was leaving him and Wyoming to go to New York City to pursue a singing career on Broadway.

They had been spoken for ever since high school, when Tom, tall and well-built even then, was the school quarterback. Maybe Faith thought he would embrace a pro-football career and that's why she agreed to be his girlfriend. Her father, however, old man Parker had been happy. He had three daughters, who were not interested

FOOTPRINTS IN THE SNOW

in running the family ranch, and Parker was looking for a future son-in-law who would take care of his ranch.

The sudden death of Tom's father and his newly acquired responsibilities made their dating slow down, although Tom asked Faith to marry him three times and she rejected him laughing. He took the refusals good-naturedly, thinking she needed time to mature. Although when both were close to thirty years old, he started to wonder how much more time she needed to see that they were meant to be together.

Faith going to New York City didn't upset him much. In fact, he thought it was better for her, instead of marrying and dreaming of a singing career in New York City, to have her New York experience and then to realize that it was better to live at home with him.

After she left, he drowned in work and did not have much time to ponder on their relationship. News of her was contradictory. First, he heard that she was a success, and was praised in the press for her singing. Then her sister, Dora, told him that Faith had failed and he started to hope she'd come back home. She returned

5

home alright, only not to him. She married Raul Maitland after a whirlwind courtship in Cheyenne.

He had nothing against Raul Maitland. In fact, Tom admired him for being a tough cowboy, who had to fight his way through life before becoming a wealthy rancher. Tom didn't begrudge him getting the Parker ranch added to Raul's own extensive Maitland lands. But losing beautiful Faith, the one girl Tom had loved all his life, hurt. She had told him that he was boring and not fun to be with. Well, too bad. He was the way he was. He knew how to raise his cattle and make his ranch prosper. He knew how to protect what was his and how to love a woman passionately and to be faithful to her. If this made him boring - too bad. He didn't know how to be different.

CHAPTER 1

Laramie, Wyoming, Two years later

Tom Gorman parked his truck behind the veterinary clinic and opened the door to his trailer. Gently he guided out Willow, the limping mare and taking the bridle pulled her inside the clinic, into an empty stall.

The mare was one of his favorite horses, very resilient and with a lot of heart. Last winter she saved him when he lost his sense of orientation in a blizzard. When he got lost, she found her way home. However, she was getting older and two days ago she stepped in a rabbit hole and injured her leg. Tom doctored her the best he could, applying a poultice and special liniment. Unfortunately, her leg was still swollen and she was favoring it, limping.

Tom brought her here to be seen by the vet. While he was not very sociable these days and especially not with the Maitland family, Tristan Maitland was the best vet in these parts of Wyoming. Tom was not very keen to meet or talk about his old flame Faith Parker, who had married into the Maitland family, but he was not an idiot. If anyone could make his mare well, it was Tristan. So here he was.

He patted the mare affectionately on the neck and she bobbed her head understanding he was doing his best to help her.

"Is your horse sick, mister?" The childish voice startled him.

A kid no older than five poked his blond head inside the stall looking at the mare with interest in his baby blue eyes. The mare stepped back and Tom tightened his grip on the bridle trying to soothe the animal. What were the parents doing that kids roamed free through the stalls of sick or wounded animals – he wondered. But what did he know about raising kids? His dreams of getting married and having a family went to dust when... Eh, ancient history.

"Does your father know where you are, kid?" he asked in a gruff tone, maybe harsher than he intended.

"He left us a year ago," the little boy said with tears in his eyes, his lower lip trembling.

Tom felt like an ogre. He didn't mean to upset the boy reminding him of the no-good father that abandoned his family.

The boy sighed. A deep, heartfelt sigh. "Mama said he went to heaven. I'm praying every night he might come back. I promised I'll be good…"

"Not many people come back from there, I'm sorry," Tom answered with compassion. Poor kid. So young and an orphan. "Rest assured your dad is watching over you like a guardian angel."

Just then they were interrupted by another boy, slightly older, about seven years old. "Billy, where are you? Uncle TJ said we have to go now…" He stopped abruptly. "Is this your horse mister?" He looked at Willow with such awe like she'd won the Kentucky Derby, not stepped into a rabbit hole and injured her leg.

Tom patted his mare one more time and left the stall closing the door. "Yes, she's mine. By the way I'm Tom Gorman, and who might you two be? Last I heard

Tristan had a little baby girl and his son Zach is twelve."

The older boy stepped forward and straightened. "I'm Wyatt Donovan Jr. and this is my brother Billy."

"Nice to meet you." Tom looked from one to the other. They looked as alike as two peas in a pod, except that the older one had hazel eyes instead of blue. "So what are you two boys doing here? I hope Tristan told you not to enter a stall or open a cage with a sick animal inside."

"Yes, he did. We know that. We come here sometimes with our uncle TJ when he needs to talk to the vet. We like to look at animals. We hope to get a puppy for Christmas." He sniffed his nose. "Maybe not this year. Mama said that we grow like weeds and coats and shoes are more important."

"If she allows you to have a dog, I have a mixed breed, part collie, that had puppies. You can have one. Again, if your mother agrees."

"Can we have one? For free?"

"Yes. Every boy needs a dog," Tom concluded, hoping the boys' mother was not one of those high and mighty city-girls who disliked animals. "You can come at my ranch to pick a puppy from the litter."

The two boys jumped up and down laughing in delight.

"Do you have horses also?" the younger boy wanted to know, his eyes lighting up with mischief. Just like Tom's did when he had been a boy planning a new adventure.

"Of course he has. He's a rancher," Wyatt answered in Tom's place. "You see, we live here in the city with our mom, and..." He looked at his brother who nodded. "We would like to learn to ride. Do you think when we come to pick up the puppy we could also ride one of the horses?"

"Not a very wild one," Billy added, excited, but also worried by this new idea.

"Of course we'll pay for the lesson. Uncle TJ gave me three dollars last week and I had some change before. That is almost five dollars. Do you think it is enough?" Wyatt asked shuffling his feet.

They were so cute in all their planning to ride a

horse. Riding. Every boy in Wyoming born on a ranch took for granted the fact that he'd get on a horse practically before learning to walk. Tom felt a desire to protect them, these two fatherless boys, looking at him with honest eyes, eager to learn to ride.

"Willow here," he said pointing at the mare, who twitched her ears hearing her name. "…she is the gentlest horse I have. After the vet helps heal her swollen leg, you two can come to the ranch and ride with me. How about that? And you can keep your money. It will do her good to exercise her leg in an easy way. What do you say?"

"Oh, thank you mister… ah, Tom. Thank you."

"Here you are, you two. I thought I lost you and your mama will have my head for this." TJ Lomax, the local private investigator was a friend of the veterinarian and he visited the clinic often with his golden retriever aptly named Goldie. "Goldie is good to go, so why don't you two run upfront where she is with Trish, the receptionist. Wait for me there."

"TJ, I thought you were a crusty old bachelor like me," Tom said looking after the two departing boys.

"What's the story with these two?"

"Tom, it's good to see you." TJ shook Tom's hand. "You are a rare bird in town or at social events." He scratched his overgrown beard. "These two boys belong to Lottie Donovan. She was in your class in high school. Do you remember her?" He chuckled answering his own question. "No, I guess not. You had eyes only for the beautiful, talented Faith Parker. And who can blame you? Anyhow, Lottie was an orphan, shuffled from a foster care home to another. A bit shy and introverted, but always believing in the goodness of people and in happy endings. She is the same today, although there was no happy end for her."

"What happened? The boys said their father died."

TJ nodded. "A year and a half ago. He was a policeman. Not from these parts. He was from Texas and from a rich family."

"What's a rich Texan doing here policing?" Tom wondered.

"I didn't say he was rich, only his family. I think

he decided to try life on his own. He was hired as a policeman here when he met Lottie. Marrying her was the last straw for his family who disowned him. He and Lottie and the two boys were quite happy together. Not rich, but happy. A year and a half ago, Wyatt stopped two robbers at the bank. He shot one of them, but was killed by the second one who ran away. A tragedy. The whole town showed up at the funeral. The youngest boy, Billy was not yet four and kept asking when his dad was coming back."

"Are they related to you?"

"No. But I worked all my life with kids in foster care to prevent abuse. Lottie likes to call me uncle. I don't mind. I help by watching the boys now and then. It's not easy for her to be a single working parent."

"They want a puppy and to learn to ride," Tom mentioned. "It's what every boy their age wants."

"Hmm, I don't think Lottie can afford either. Money is tight with only her teacher's income and she's proud. She won't accept charity."

"Riding is free at my ranch and a puppy can eat

scraps from the table. Dogs didn't always have such a large variety of canned and bagged foods or toys," Tom explained.

The door of one of the rooms opened and Tristan Maitland, the veterinarian came to them. "Tom, I haven't seen you in a while. I hope you're coming next week to Old Man Maitland's birthday party. He's 70 years old. It will be a big party. All the neighbors are invited. You're coming, aren't you?"

To go to the Maitland house and pretend to be merry? Not if he could avoid it. "I might be busy, you know," Tom hedged.

"Busy. It's winter. You can take a break, I'm sure."

TJ added his objection too. "You used to be the soul of every party, Tom. A real Wyoming cowboy. Hard working, but also knowing how to party and dance. Now, look at you. You've become a real hermit."

"Yes, you have to come," Tristan said. "You have to see my little angel. Miranda is one year old. Thank the good Lord she looks like her mother, not like me. She has Eleanor's blond hair and blue eyes. She's a marvel," he said full of paternal pride.

Another reason not to go to the party, Tom thought. He heard Faith had given birth to a boy. It reminded Tom of his single and childless state.

"Ah, this pretty lady is Willow," Tristan said entering the horse's stall.

"She stepped into a rabbit hole two days ago and her leg is swollen. The poultice and liniment didn't help much," Tom explained, but Tristan was not paying attention. He was whispering some words to the mare soothing her and slowly touching the injured leg.

Both Tom and TJ watched the veterinarian who, like a magician worked his spell on the horse.

"I swear he's a wizard when it comes to animals. He has a magic touch," TJ said. He caught Tom's arm. "Listen, I thought of what you said about the boys. You are right. They need a dog and riding lessons like any other boy their age. Lottie is frazzled these days. Mourning Wyatt, working as a teacher, and being a mother to two energetic, active boys. I appreciate your offer to help the boys. Frankly I was worried for Lottie. Here is their address." TJ pressed in Tom's hand a piece of paper.

By the time Tom thought to protest that he rarely came to town, TJ had left and Tom looked at the paper again. Hmm, Lottie Donovan. He was sure he knew no one from high school with this name, but somehow it sounded familiar.

CHAPTER 2

It was late and Lottie was tired. The boys were in bed sleeping and hopefully having nice dreams. Billy had not accepted that his father passed away and at times woke up from nightmares crying.

Lottie rubbed her eyes and started to add again. The result was the same and she had to face the truth. This large new house had been a stretch for their finances even with two incomes. Wyatt had wanted to buy it, hoping he'd be promoted soon and be able to afford the mortgage. The promotion didn't happen and they had to stretch their resources even more. Now Lottie had to admit the truth. She could not make the hefty mortgage payments from her teacher's income. She tried to supplement it by working two nights a week as a cook at a truck stop at the edge of town. Not the safest area, but as they say 'beggars can't be choosers'. Besides, it had the advantage that she could go any day she wanted when she had a babysitter for the boys. Also, Carrie Ingram who had a bakery shop in town was selling goods baked by Lottie, her cupcakes and cookies were very much in demand. This helped the money problem, but didn't solve it.

Working more nights at the truck stop would mean paying more for a babysitter. And Lottie hated staying away from her children. She was meant to be a mother and a housewife, not a breadwinner. Silently she raged against fate who took Wyatt away and against Wyatt who had to be a hero and got himself killed. Furiously she wiped her tears. Crying or raging against injustice never helped in a constructive way to solve one's problems. As an orphan she knew that better than anyone.

She had to sell the house. She hated to do that, to sell the dream house that Wyatt wanted, planning their future in it. But Wyatt was no more and bills had to be paid. Uprooting the boys from the only home they had known was cruel. After they lost their father they were to lose their home too. But it couldn't be helped.

As a child raised in foster care homes, Lottie swore her children would never know the humiliation of wearing hand-me-down clothes and scuffed shoes. The kids were growing fast and they needed a lot of things. Right now most of her income went toward paying the mortgage.

She had to call the realtor to place the house on the market. Having made her decision, Lottie went to the kitchen to bake a hundred cupcakes to take to the bakery the next day.

Tom questioned his sanity and his decision to come here and bring the puppy with him. The house was rather new and had a For Sale sign on the front lawn. Tom consulted the piece of paper TJ Lomax had given him. The address was correct. So, why was the house listed for sale?

The puppy squirmed inside his winter jacket and he patted it gently. The puppy whined, but quieted for the moment.

Leaving his truck in front of the house, Tom went to the front door. He raised his hand to ring the bell when the door opened and a frazzled looking blonde, short and well-rounded got out. She was carrying a large box, balancing her keys in one of her hands under the box.

Everything happened at once.

"Oh, oh," she said when she hit him in the chest with the box.

"Let me help you," he said, trying to support the box with one of his hands.

And the puppy yipped inside his jacket.

The box fell to the ground.

"My cupcakes," the blonde cried and tears flooded her eyes.

Not knowing what to do, he gathered her in his arms and awkwardly patted her back. Surprisingly, she fit quite nicely, all curves and soft. The puppy, not knowing what the commotion was about, chose that moment to push his head outside Tom's coat.

"Oh," she said again. And she smiled through tears. "Aren't you a darling?" she cooed at the puppy who tried to lick her cheek. He squirmed and came out of Tom's jacket into her arms. "Come in," she said while cuddling the little dog.

21

Tom looked down and picked up the now rather deformed box. The squishy noise inside warned him that the cupcakes were probably a lost cause, but maybe one or two remained intact.

Once inside, Tom was attacked by two energetic little boys, very happy to see him. "Mister Tom, you came to take us riding, yes?" the older one asked eagerly.

"Did you come to help us move? Our house sold and we have to move," the younger one announced jumping up and down.

"Mama said that a larger family with more children will move into our house. We could have more kids in the family. I wouldn't mind. Then we could stay here," Wyatt, the older said frowning.

The puppy decided he wanted to play and have fun with the kids and yipped.

"Boys," Lottie said. "This little guy belongs to Mr. Gorman. You can play with him a little before giving him back."

"But Mama, he brought it for us to keep," Billy protested.

Lottie turned to Tom. "You did? When...?"

"Last week at the vet. TJ assured me that you wouldn't mind," Tom answered wondering what trouble he had gotten himself into this time.

She placed her hand on her forehead, looked at the boys playing with the dog. "It's not that I mind, but a dog is another responsibility...." She sighed. "I guess he can stay. Thank you."

Tom started to understand the problem. "Why are you selling the house, Lottie?" he asked straightforward.

"The house is too big for us now, without Wyatt and..." she gave the usual explanation. But Tom was still looking at her expectantly, waiting for the real reason. So, almost against her good sense and pride, she blurted out the truth. "I'm a teacher and a single parent. I can't afford the payments." She covered her mouth with her hand. Why did she confess this to Tom of all people? Yet, somehow it felt right to unburden the source of her daily worries to him.

He nodded in understanding. Lottie looked at him smiling. "You don't remember me, do you?"

"TJ said we were in the same class in high school," he answered somewhat embarrassed not to remember a classmate from high school, but this was the truth. For the life of him he could not remember her. In fact, there were a lot of fuzzy faces of people less important in his life at the time. He looked at her. What he saw was a frumpy full-figured woman, with a head full of honey colored curls, caught in a topknot. Maybe released from the tie her hair could make her look prettier. She had lines of worry on her forehead and her beautiful hazel eyes expressed a world of hurt, worry, and fatigue. Nope, he didn't remember her.

"I was Charlotte Evans in high school," she said.

These words triggered a 'deja vue' or heard memory. Indeed he heard this before. He couldn't recall when. He shook his head.

"I understand and I'm not offended," she said amused by his predicament. "You had eyes only for Faith then."

That was the problem with coming to town and socializing. Every person needed to remind him of his unfortunate love for Faith Parker.

"She is a wonderful person," Lottie continued. "Not only very beautiful and talented, but brave and loyal and a wonderful friend."

"Not very loyal to me," Tom muttered.

Lottie clutched his hand. "Be honest, Tom. Did she promise or agree to anything and then reneged on her word? No, you don't have to tell me. Just think."

Then she looked at the deformed box on the table. She opened it carefully and picked a cupcake less damaged. Placing it on a small plate she brought it to him. "Here. It will sweeten your thoughts."

"I don't need…" Realizing how churlish he sounded he accepted her offering. "Thank you." The taste of vanilla and some spice in a moist cake with a lemony creamy icing melted in his mouth. "Mmm, this is divine." He ate his cupcake in a few bites and gave her back the plate only to find it filled again with a chocolaty concoction. His mouth watered only looking at it. "You know Lottie, I apologize for ruining the little cakes. Let me make it up to you and buy some more. Where did you get these?"

"You don't have to. I made them," she answered simply. "I like to bake. I was taking them to Carrie Ingram from the bakery shop."

"It's her birthday?" he asked, wiping his mouth with the napkin and wondering if he could ask for the pinkish one with a lopsided top. He'd bet it was strawberry flavored and that was his favorite.

Lottie laughed. "No. She's so kind and sells them in her store. It's an extra hundred dollars a week for me."

"Oh, I see." He started to get the picture of Lottie's hard times since her husband's death.

"I have always liked to cook. It helps now. In fact, I work two nights a week or when I need extra money as a cook at the truck stop near I80."

"You do?" Tom was horrified. He knew that particular diner and it was frequented by rough people.

"Yes, but I'm hoping that once I won't have such a huge mortgage payment I'll be all right with only my teacher's income. Of course during the breaks, I'll have to find additional work."

"Where are you moving?"

"I'm not sure. When I listed the house three days ago, the realtor warned me that the winter, especially near Christmas is not a good time to sell a house. In other words the season in real estate is dead. People are busy with the holidays. Come back in spring or summer. So I thought I had a lot of time to find a smaller place for us. But this young couple just moved into town and they needed the house fast. So you see, in a way I was lucky to sell, but now we are homeless. TJ, our guardian angel, invited us to live with him until I find another place."

"Wait!" Tom paused with his third - or was it the fourth - cupcake midair. "I thought TJ lived in a studio above his office."

Lottie nodded. "Yes. In fact it is a small one bedroom apartment, but I am grateful and hope to find something else quickly. I don't know what else to do. I could go live at the Maitland ranch. Faith offered too. But Little Elliott is not a year old and…I wouldn't want to be in the way."

"Surely not," Tom exclaimed. For some strange

reason, he didn't want Lottie to go live with the
Maitlands. Although where Lottie lived, was not his
business. Yet, he was bothered by this. He looked at the
pink creamy bite in his hand. Ah, good! After
swallowing slowly, he turned to Lottie. "I have a better
idea. I have a large house and it's just my sister Brianna,
my brother Chris and I. All three of us bachelors. You
could move to stay temporarily with us. There is plenty
of space for all of us. The county school bus stops at the
main road. And the boys wanted to learn to ride. It will
be a good experience for them to see life on the ranch
until you find a better place to move permanently."

Lottie opened her mouth, looked at him with wide
eyes in surprise. "Tom, I can't inconvenience you. Lord,
you don't even know me. Why would you offer to house
us?"

"Of course I know you. We were in high school
together, remember?" he said, snatching another
cupcake, this one with a mystery creamy green top. Tom
couldn't think of any green desert but he decided to be
adventurous and to give it a try.

Lottie laughed. "In high school, you were the heroic quarterback all girls dreamed about, who had a homecoming queen girlfriend, while I was the shy, chubby girl, wearing hand-me-down clothes, always with my nose in a book." She shook her head. "No, Tom, you are very generous, but I can't accept."

The green thing, whatever it was, was delicious. Tom's mind was made up. He took her hand. "Lottie, my housekeeper, who raised Brie and me, had to go to Cheyenne to take care of a cousin who broke her leg. Unfortunately, she was also our cook and now we take turns in the kitchen. It's one disaster after another other."

She smiled. "That bad?"

"Let's just say, Chris is the only one who knows how to make scrambled eggs, but not much else."

"What about your sister?"

"Are you kidding? Brianna is one of the best cowboys I have, but in the kitchen she is helpless. So I was thinking that if you could make some cupcakes from time to time, it will be great."

It seemed that not many people had ever helped

29

Lottie in life and she found it difficult to accept.

"I don't know..." She looked at the two boys laughing and playing with the puppy. For them it would be heaven to live on the ranch for a while. Was she wrong to accept? Tom was looking at her, friendly, full of compassion, a little green dot at the corner of his mouth. What could she say? "Yes. Thank you."

CHAPTER 3

Classes were over and Lottie left school smiling. For the first time since Wyatt died, she didn't feel the overwhelming responsibility weighing on her shoulders, the pressure to raise the boys all alone.

Selling the house was the right financial decision, and maybe not only financial. It was a place full of memories, good ones, happy ones, but it was time to move on and build a new life. Tom's offer to house them until they found a permanent place to live had been a miracle. The boys needed a little excitement to release their young energy and it would be a great life experience for them to live on the ranch.

For her part, Lottie swore to give the Gormans the best meals they ever tasted and because Christmas was near, to decorate and make a memorable celebration for them all.

Lost in thought, she bumped into a man who walked in the opposite direction. "Sorry!" she said but the words remained stuck in her throat. Doug Williams, her old nemesis from a time better forgotten. The son of her foster parents. A bully who resented all the children that his parents fostered, conveniently ignoring the fact that his parents, most of the time jobless, needed the money the state paid them for taking care of these orphans.

"Well, well, if this isn't little Charlotte…," the man said in a nasal voice, leering at her.

Lottie didn't answer, trying to continue on her way.

He grabbed her arm, stopping her. "What? Now you are too high and mighty to talk to me? I remember a time when you came begging into our house."

"I didn't come begging. I was sent to live with you by the Social Services. I had no choice."

"You ungrateful little…" A calculating look came in his eyes. "Hmm, I heard your husband got himself killed."

Lottie raised her chin. "My husband was a hero."

He shrugged. "Hero or no hero, dead is dead. I thought by now you'd be in desperate need of male company." He laughed revealing yellowish bad teeth.

"Not that desperate, no."

"You can't tell me no. It's not like you changed into a swan overnight. You're the same mousy fat girl you have been before. I don't see many men knocking on your door. You should be glad old Doug here is willing to close his eyes at night and do the deed."

Lottie closed her eyes in humiliation. The words hurt even coming from a revolting toad like Doug. "Let go of me!" she cried trying to snatch back her arm.

"Lottie, here you are. I thought you'd left earlier." Never had Lottie been so happy to see someone like now. Faith Parker Maitland approached them and raised her eyebrow haughtily at Doug. Surprised he stepped back. Stunningly beautiful and regal, Faith looked down her nose at him. "Lottie dear, do you have anything to talk with this person?"

"N-no," Lottie said fervently.

Faith narrowed her eyes. "You heard her. Now, beat it."

Doug opened his mouth to protest then changed

his mind and turned away hurriedly.

Lottie hugged her friend. "Oh, Faith, you are so brave and fearless. I wish I could be like you."

"Nonsense. You are brave to raise two little boys and to face life's hardship alone. Who was this person? He looked unkempt."

"My last foster parents had a biological son who was a bully. We were three girls fostered there and he was mean and he pinched us all the time. We had to steer clear of him."

"This guy."

"Yep, this is the one. I heard he spent some time in prison…" Lottie looked faraway, sad, then shook her head to chase the bad memories away. "He is not important anymore."

Faith was skeptical. "I don't know. His kind seems to pop up like a bad weed when you don't expect. Anyhow, I'm glad you're coming to live with us. You'll be safe."

"What? No, Faith, I don't want to inconvenience you and Raul. Besides another offer came out of the blue." She looked at her friend shyly wondering if Faith might disapprove of her going to live at the Diamond G ranch. "Tom Gorman was so kind to invite us to live at his ranch until I find a permanent place to live."

"Tom 'the recluse' Gorman? He invited you to live with him?" Faith asked surprised.

"He's not a recluse, only very busy and hard-working." Lottie defended Tom.

"In his twenties, he was the soul of the party, the best dancer in three counties. His father's death affected him deeply, not to mention all the new responsibilities," Faith remembered.

"And the loss of his longtime sweetheart," Lottie supplied tongue in cheek.

"Lottie, I was always honest with Tom that I wanted to be a professional singer and that I would leave Wyoming to achieve this. He was never very upset by it. Besides there was never that passion between us, like when you see him, you feel like melting into a puddle. I know that passion now because I feel it for Raul. Never for Tom."

"How could you not? He is the most handsome man in these parts of Wyoming. When we were in high school all the girls were in love with our quarterback. He was splendid and he had eyes only for you to the disappointment of all the girls." Lottie smiled wistfully.

"Were you one of them Lottie?" Faith asked half joking, but scrutinizing her friend with attention.

Lottie shrugged. "All girls that age have dreams. Unlike others who had also hopes, I didn't. I was an overweight girl, poorly dressed in second hand clothes. I had more realistic goals, like how to save every penny to go to college or to study hard to get a scholarship. Of course I admired Tom, but I had no time to waste on foolish dreams. Life in foster care taught me better."

"Oh Lottie, was there no one willing to adopt you?" Faith asked full of compassion.

"No. I had an uncle, my mother's brother. I was six when my parents died. He took a look at me and said 'No way. This pudgy girl will eat me out of my house.' And he never tried to contact me again. Maybe it was for the best. He had two girls older than me who were not very kind. I'd have been Cinderella in their house. And real life doesn't end like the fairy tales. I'd have ended up as an unpaid servant in their house, maybe not even able to go to college."

"Was his wife the wicked stepmother?"

"No. If I recall correctly the social worker wrote - sickly wife can't take on the care of another child.... But let's talk about something else. Tom said his housekeeper went to Cheyenne to take care of a cousin. And no one cooks in his family. That was the deal. He liked my cupcakes and wants me to bake him some. He also promised the boys to teach them to ride. I'm not sure it's entirely safe for them, but I trust Tom and I have to let them be boys, no matter how protective I want to be."

Faith laughed. "Do you think my heart doesn't somersault when Raul takes Elliott in front of him in the saddle? But Elliott chortles with glee and raises his little fist in the air and I swallow even the 'take care' words that I want to tell Raul."

"In the saddle. Surely not. Elliott is not yet one year old. Does he walk?"

Faith nodded. "Since he was nine months old. He couldn't wait to explore his surroundings."

"Oh Faith, they grow up so fast… I hope they'll be safe on the ranch."

"Sure. Tom is a very careful rancher. Of course there is Brianna, who's horse mad and Chris who is… strange. But don't worry, Tom will take good care of the boys."

"How old is his sister?"

"About three years younger than us. Twenty-eight, twenty-nine. She liked horses ever since she was a little girl. She works together with the cowboys on the range. That ranch is her life, although Daddy, the old man Gorman, decided otherwise. He left the entire ranch, land, house, and livestock to Tom. He left Brianna a large amount of money. To add insult to injury, he mentioned in his will that this money is to entice some worthy man to marry her. Don't you love these old fashioned men who think that a woman needs a dowry to get married? Brianna proved all her life that she is a good rancher. Unfortunately, there was a tragic love story in her teenage years – I don't know the details – and she withdrew from the social life, preferring to work on the range."

"How about the other brother, Chris? Didn't he get a part of the ranch?"

"Now that is a mystery. He didn't get anything simply because old man Gorman had no idea he existed. One day after the old man passed away, Chris came to Tom and announced they were brothers. He is a weird one and also prefers the company of animals instead of humans. Tom doesn't talk about him, but he accepted him into the family. That's why I'm surprised Tom invited you to live with them. They are a strange bunch and don't like to mix with others. They were not always like this. But now…"

Lottie was overwhelmed, but also intrigued by Tom's family. "All families have secrets and stories better left untold."

Faith agreed. "True. The Maitlands had a whole drama hidden in the family history. Not to mention weird people," she said thinking of her own sister.

An older woman with salt and pepper hair came out of the school. Ms. Proffitt was principal of the school and their math teacher from their high school days. "Girls, you'd think that after a whole day in school you have finished imparting all the gossipy news worth telling. Don't you think you could leave some for tomorrow and go home?"

"Yes, Ms. Proffitt," they chorused together like they did in high school. Then burst into laughter.

The principal shook her head and left smiling.

"She didn't use to smile in high school," Faith said looking after the principal.

Lottie came closer and whispered, "She is keeping company with my uncle TJ Lomax these days, working on a charity project together," she said and winked at Faith.

They dissolved into peals of laughter again.

CHAPTER 4

The furniture was placed in storage. Three suitcases containing their clothes and other things they needed in this transitional stay at the ranch and a few mementos that Lottie could not part with, all was packed in the car and they said their Goodbyes to the house where their family had lived for several years and where the boys had grown up.

Another family would move in the next day. And Lottie would look for a smaller place. She thought even a small apartment would do, but now with the new addition of Tiger, the puppy, they needed a house with a yard. She hoped it would be within her budget or she'd have to go back to cooking at the truck stop.

It was a sunny, crisp, and very cold winter morning. Lottie loved Wyoming in winter. The wide open spaces with patches of snow here and there and the straight road, a ribbon of asphalt in front of them as far as one could see to the horizon. The air was crisp and invigorating. A new beginning.

41

Lottie felt energetic, despite finding a paper on her windshield this morning scribbled with black marker, "I'll find you". It was probably a prank from one of the neighbor's kids. She found a local station playing Christmas carols and she started singing along. The boys hummed with her and even Tiger was yipping now and again. They'll be fine, she encouraged herself.

"Look, Mama, the Diamond G ranch to the right," Wyatt said, bouncing on his seat.

Lottie turned right on the country road where a large sign announced they were on Gorman land. The main house was indeed large, as Tom had told them, a true ranch house, with additions made by generations past.

"And horses," Billy chimed in happily, pointing to some horses in the distance.

Lottie stopped the car and she helped the boys out, cautioning them not to let the puppy loose, until they talked to Tom.

A tall lanky cowboy, with his Stetson pulled low on his head, came from the barn and passed by them going to the house.

"Excuse me," Lottie said after him, "Could you tell me where…" Her words died down when he ignored them and entered in the house, closing the front door firmly after him. "Well, well, that was not nice," Lottie muttered, wondering again if maybe coming here was a mistake after all.

They were all three at the front entrance when the door opened and they came face to face with a woman on her way out. "Who are you?" she asked looking at Lottie.

"Hello, I'm Lottie Donovan and these are my children Wyatt and Billy. Could you please tell me where I could find Tom?"

"Tom is busy with a sick calf. You'll have to tell me what your business is with Tom," she said curtly, without bothering to introduce herself.

Not an auspicious welcome and Lottie considered again turning around. But she was already here and she did not have many options. "We sold our house recently and ….it sold overnight and the buyers wanted to move in right away and…Tom was so nice to invite us to live at his ranch until we find a place to live."

"Tom invited you to live here? You've got to be kidding." The woman shook her head in disbelief. "Tom would never do a foolish thing like that."

"Well, he did." Lottie understood how this woman, probably Tom's sister Brianna, might not be happy to have guests all of a sudden. "Could we talk to Tom?"

"No. I thought he learned his lesson after that heartless witch, Faith Parker made a fool of him."

"Faith is not heartless and she had never made any promises to him," Lottie argued, defending Faith.

"Ah, so you know her."

"Faith is my best friend," Lottie admitted.

Brianna scoffed. "It figures. Did she send you here? Did she tell you that Tom is a sucker for lost strays?"

Wyatt stepped in front of Lottie. "Don't you talk to my mother that way. Mr. Tom invited us to come here, but we don't have to stay if we're not wanted."

Lottie felt like crying. Wyatt, her knight in

shinning armor. She looked at Billy who was holding tightly to her hand and his other hand had his thumb in his mouth, a habit he had outgrown except for moments when he was scared or felt insecure.

"Why would Tom invite you to live here?" Brianna repeated.

"He came to bring our puppy to us and he liked Mama's cupcakes. He hoped Mama would bake some more if we came to live here," Wyatt explained before Lottie could.

"Darn Tom and his sweet tooth. Couldn't he buy cakes from town?"

"No, ma'am. Not as good as my Mama' s," Wyatt informed her.

Brianna measured her with interest. "Are you a cook then?"

"No, I'm a high school teacher," Lottie explained with a calm she didn't feel. "Tom invited us to stay here temporary until we find a place to live. I am however a good cook and I know my way around a kitchen."

"Look, there is Tom," Wyatt interrupted them.

Tom was coming from the barn. He looked tired and his hair disheveled. He wore no hat. Lottie had never seen a more handsome man in her life. She had loved her husband and had been devoted to him. They had a good marriage and a good life together, albeit too short. Yet Tom was the one she had admired from high school and always considered him the ideal man, handsome, hard-working, warm-hearted.

He smiled when he saw them. "You came. Good, good. Why are you standing on the porch? Let's get in. It's cold out here. I wouldn't be surprised to see snow tonight." He gestured to his sister to step aside and ushered them inside.

Like many houses in the area, the large living room had a massive stone fireplace and was warm if not inviting. A pleasant change to the freezing cold outside.

"Where are your manners Brie? You should have asked them in," Tom chastised his sister, then turned to Lottie. "I don't know if you've been introduced. This here is my baby sister Brianna. And there…," he gestured to the far corner of the room where the tall lanky cowboy, they first met, was leaning against the door his arms crossed, looking at them. "…That is my brother Chris, a rather new addition to our family."

"He sure grew fast for a newborn," Billy observed.

Tom laughed ruffling the boy's hair. "He was born twenty-eight years ago. He came to meet us recently."

The cowboy came closer looking from one to the other.

"Nice to meet you, Chris," Lottie said bending to take off Billy's jacket. "I'm Lottie Donovan and these are…"

"Ma'am," Chris interrupted her. "Please look at me when you are talking so I can read your lips."

Lottie straightened. "Oh, you can't hear."

He shrugged. "I hear some, just not very well. I lost partially my hearing when I was sixteen after a nasty bout of flu. With hearing aids I can manage, but I need to see the lips of the person speaking." He smiled. A charming roguish smile so similar to Tom's it was obvious they were brothers.

Lottie smiled back. "Agreed, Chris."

Billy pulled at her jeans to get her attention. "Mama, Tiger is still in the car. Can I go to let him out?"

Tom looked at his brother. "Chris, could you please go with them? Tiger is the puppy from our collie's litter." He turned to Lottie who was looking with apprehension after her boys, who went out with Chris. "Don't worry, because he can't hear Chris will keep an eye on them all the time. They'll be fine."

Brianna came from the kitchen with a tray with hot coffee. She set it on the table. "Sorry we're out of treats. We didn't expect guests. Tom didn't say a word." She grabbed her jacket and left the house in a huff, pulling the door shut with more force than necessary.

"Sorry for Brie. She has been out of sorts since Dad died," Tom said in the awkward silence that followed.

Lottie placed her hand on his arm. "Tom, I appreciate very much your kind offer to give us shelter until I'll find us a house, but I don't want to cause discord in your family. I think it would be better if we left."

He covered her hand with his own and a wave of warmth suffused Lottie's whole body. "What discord? Brie has been acting surly for a long time and Chris is all right. He has his own issues that he needs to sort out, but he's a great guy considering all the challenges he faced in his life and I don't mean only his hearing disability. So you see, Lottie we are a dysfunctional family and we need someone to whip us in shape. I don't know exactly how or even if it's possible. I know only that the three of us are not at peace. We are surviving, busy with work, but we are not enjoying life. And I miss the time in my childhood when my mother was alive and the house was full of laughter...."

Yes, Lottie understood very well. She probably couldn't do a thing about their personal peace of mind. What she could do, however, in the short time that she lived here was to create a home for them. A home with children's laughter and silly jokes, with dogs playing, a warm fire in the fireplace, a house smelling of good food and with a permanent supply of cookies. She could envision this and she could do it if Tom allowed her.

"This is a beautiful house, Tom. It's already December, when do you plan to decorate for Christmas?"

Tom frowned like it had never occurred to him to bring in a Christmas tree. "I don't think we planned," he confessed sheepishly. "You see, we are all busy and Mariah is in Cheyenne, so there is no one to do it."

"What about Brianna?"

"Brie is the least of us inclined to decorate. She can rope a steer or ride better than any cowboy, but decorate? No way. To my chagrin she is not even into all the girlie froufrou, you know, dresses, make-up and such." He scratched his head, tousling his light brown hair some more. "I was hoping with another woman in the house she'll change too. I saw your house and I was hoping you'll take a hand to change things here."

"Do I have your permission to decorate and improve around here?" Lottie asked already envisioning some necessary changes.

"Lottie, please do whatever you want to make this

house alive again."

CHAPTER 5

Lord, I sound pathetic, Tom thought. And why was he confessing to this woman, practically a stranger, things about himself and his family that he never did when he was with Faith? The truth was that Faith used to talk only about her grand plans of a singing career and never paid much attention to Tom's feelings. So Tom kept his thoughts to himself. He had thought at the time that Faith was a precious beauty to be admired and not burdened with his worries about the ranch and his family.

Looking into Lottie's hazel eyes full of compassion, he saw not pity, but the understanding of a person who carried a lot of scars herself. That's why it was so easy to talk to her. Because he felt she understood him.

"This is all the family I have and I can't reach them. We're all three alone and we can't find comfort in each other," he continued. "Brianna has closed herself from the world. She is permanently upset, huffing and puffing and pushing me away. Chris is smiling and agreeing and under this agreeable mask he hides his pain. I can't reach them and I can't make them happy, Lottie."

She came closer. "You can't make anyone happy. Only they can do that. You can only give comfort and support."

Tom raised his hand and touched her blond curls. "Are you happy Lottie?" Then he remembered that she lost her husband a year and a half ago. "I'm sorry, I'm an insensitive clod."

"No, you are not. I'm trying to be happy. When I was a little girl I used to pray my parents would come back, until I understood they would not. Then I prayed someone would adopt me and I'd be part of a loving family. When that didn't happen either, I finally understood that my happiness is up to me."

"Did you give up your dreams?" he asked hurting for the little girl she had been, alone in the world.

"Only the impossible, unrealistic ones," Lottie said, touching his cheek. "I made myself as unobtrusive as I could so as not to provoke the anger of my foster family. Life was not easy in foster care. I tried to be invisible. When I was eighteen I made plans of my own. These were possible dreams. To finish college, to be a teacher, and to have a family of my own. And I achieved all this."

People tended to dismiss Lottie, especially when in the company of her friend Faith who stole the show with her beauty and poise. Tom realized that in reality Lottie was a very strong person. This short, funny woman went through a lot in life and was still facing hardship, good-natured and smiling.

"It's not easy to lose a loved one. You know that." Lottie looked at him and because she was close he placed his arms around her. She nestled there like a kitten.

"Did you love him?"

"Yes. He was a good husband and we had a happy marriage. It was not easy. Money was tight, mainly because the house payments were almost too much with our incomes. Wyatt hoped he'd be promoted. I have been accustomed all my life with little money, so we were happy. The boys were healthy. Everything was great until Wyatt got killed. Then I almost collapsed, but I didn't have that luxury. The boys needed constant comfort. Billy had nightmares, so I survived. Then there were other challenges. I informed his family of his death and I don't think they cared very much, but they assumed they could come and take the boys. Just like that, like they were objects."

"What did you do?"

"I informed them that I'll contact every newspaper in Texas to tell them how the rich Donovan family treated their son's widow and children."

"You think this will keep them at bay?"

"Maybe. I hope his sister will have kids of her own. She was not able last time I talked to them."

"Lottie, life was not easy for you…"

"I don't complain. We are all in good health. I have a job I like. I wish I could spend more time with the boys, but as a single mom I have to work. We'll be fine," she concluded, rubbing her cheek on his shirt. "We'll all be fine, don't worry."

She was an armful of feminine curves nestled

against him. She felt warm and cuddly and Tom was strangely aroused. No, surely not by Lottie Donovan. He liked his women tall and regal like Faith. Although he didn't remember that Faith's nearness had ever stirred him like this. He willed his body into submission and breathed deeply. This brought into his nostrils a flowery smell with hints of vanilla and his body reacted some more.

"I'm sorry I have to go back to the barn," he muttered to hide his embarrassment.

Lottie looked at him confused for a moment. Then she disentangled her hand from his shirt where she had opened his first two buttons. "Right, of course. You have to go."

Tom stepped back and cursed himself for a fool. "Lottie, I …you…Feel free to decorate the house in any way you want." He turned to go.

"Wait. My boys are still out there," she cried.

"Don't worry. They are among cowboys. I'll watch over them. Nothing will happen."

After he left, Lottie sat in the nearest chair and

looked around. She was alone in a strange house where she had never been before. And she had a purpose, to bring this family together and to transform this house into a home. She could do that for Tom. It would be awkward at first with Brianna so set to think the worst of Lottie but she could do it. Her boys would be fine romping with the cowboys. And if she were to succeed, she had to avoid getting so close to Tom. That had been embarrassing and the poor man couldn't run outside faster.

Lottie's contemplation was interrupted when the door opened with a bang and a tall, large cowboy came in carrying Lottie's suitcases.

"Howdy ma'am. Pardon for not taking off my hat," he said from under the mountain of luggage. "Where do you want these?"

Lottie was taken aback. She had no idea what room Tom intended them to occupy. "I don't know. In one of the guest bedrooms I suppose."

The cowboy grunted in agreement and marched somewhere down the hallway. He certainly knew better than Lottie where the bedrooms where.

Sighing Lottie rolled up her sleeves and went in the kitchen where she expected a mess of dirty dishes and unwashed pots. It was surprisingly clean. Stark clean. The counters were empty of cookie jars, opened chip bags, spices, bread and other daily used groceries that usually were found on the kitchen counters. Only a single coffee maker was pushed to the wall. However opening the cabinets and the pantry she found them very well supplied with all sorts of groceries and so was the large refrigerator. She smiled relieved. It was important for all ranch houses isolated from town to have plenty of supplies to survive on their own, especially in winter.

"Ma'am." The cowboy was back, standing in the kitchen doorway. "Your things are in the two larger guest bedrooms. By the way, I'm Virgil," he said taking his hat off. "I used to work at the Parker ranch until this summer when Gimpy Fred, the foreman retired and Raul Maitland brought a team from Montana and so I moved here," he explained twisting his hat in his hands.

"You don't get along with Raul Maitland?" Lottie

asked surprised. From what she knew of Raul, she liked Faith's husband very much. He adored Faith and treated her like she was made of precious China. Wyatt had been a good husband, but he had never coddled Lottie like Raul did Faith.

"Raul is all right. It's just that many of the old cowboys left with Gimpy Fred and the guys from Montana kept to themselves. I heard that now they are friendlier. But I'm happy here and better off….Frankly I have a curious nature and when I heard Boss had brought in a pretty lady I offered to help. Boss said that I'm to help you with anything you need."

"That's very nice of you but I don't want to take you from your work."

"No problem, ma'am. Boss said to help. Tell me what you need. There are more food supplies in the cellar."

"I have all I need," Lottie thanked him smiling when an idea popped in her head. "If you have time I would like a tree and some greenery."

He scratched his head. "A tree and some bushes.

It might be difficult to plant it now in the dead of winter."

Lottie laughed. "Sorry. I want a Christmas tree. There is a place on the outskirts of town where they sell pretty ones. They have a tree farm."

He looked at her in wonder. "A Christmas tree. Could we all come and see it when it's decorated?"

"Of course. You are all invited on Christmas Day to come and share a meal with the family and sing carols. Have you been an orphan Virgil?" It could explain while a Christmas proper celebration was such a wonder for him. "And call me Lottie, please."

"No ma'am, Lottie. My Pa died when I was eight and when Ma remarried, life was not so good. No Christmas tree ever. A day without a beating was a blessing. At twelve I ran away and never looked back. I drifted through Wyoming for a while hiring to work. I figured if I had to work from morning till night it could very well be for myself. I was big for my age. I said I was sixteen and no one asked more."

"But what about school?"

"Later I hired in construction in Cheyenne and the master builder forced me to study. I got my GED diploma."

"How come you didn't stay in construction?"

"Ah, ma'am. Money was good and I set aside a little, but the open spaces of the range called to me. I came back and hired at Parker's ranch. Old man Parker was fair and treated me right. Maitland is fair too, but I prefer working for Gorman. He is more than fair, he is part of the team. A leader who works as hard as any of his men."

"Yes, he is a good man," Lottie agreed, feeling like crying all of a sudden. "He and all of you deserve a nice Christmas. And I'll see that you have it. Now Virgil, please go and bring me a nice tree and some green branches. I have ornaments and all."

Virgil's homely face lighted with a rare smile. "Yes, ma'am. Right away." He placed his hat back on his head. "I'm glad Boss brought you here. Your boys took to the saddle like ducks to water. They will make fine cowboys. Boss will see to that."

Lottie blinked wondering if Virgil knew she was there only temporary until she found a new place to live. She opened her mouth to tell him so, but he was gone.

She gathered what she needed to prepare a fine meal for dinner. And in short time the house smelled like roast beef with Lottie's special herbs and cornbread with jalapeno peppers, just a touch to give it a kick. Roasted vegetables in a garlic sauce. Then apple pie made from scratch and vanilla pudding.

CHAPTER 6

In less than two hours, Lottie had the kitchen looking and smelling very inviting, with the roast beef in the oven almost ready, the last batch of chocolate chip cookies resting on a rack near the pan of steaming cornbread. The roasted vegetables waited in the second oven to be tossed with garlic sauce at the last minute before serving so as not to become mushy and the vanilla pudding was waiting its turn for twenty minutes in the oven after the beef was ready. The apple pie was cooling on the island.

Humming, Lottie was setting the long table in the large country kitchen when the door opened and Virgil came in sniffing with relish.

"Ms. Lottie, I think I died and went to heaven. I've never smelled anything so divine in my life. Could I have a cookie?" he asked like a little boy, extending his hand toward the cookie platter.

"No Virgil," Lottie laughed pushing his hand away. "It's almost dinner time. I expect you to go wash your hands and come to the table. You can call the others too."

Virgil sighed disappointed. "We, the cowboys take our meals at the bunkhouse. Only the family dines here. Lately they came to the bunkhouse too, when Miss Brianna burnt the food, which was most of the time. Boss almost banished her from the kitchen, but he's not much better at cooking either."

"And who cooks for you?" Lottie asked curious about how the ranch was managed.

"Our foreman's wife, Rachel. She's not a bad cook, except that she cooks mostly beans with salted pork or beef with potatoes. We prefer the beans 'cause her beef is always overdone, tough and stringy. Now, there are only a few of us in the bunkhouse, Hank, the foreman, Angel and I. The rest went home for the holidays. They'll come back in January when work starts to pick up."

"Ah, I see. I expect you all to come here tonight. I'm sure Tom will have no objections to this invitation. He left me in charge of the house, so please come." As an additional inducement, Lottie grabbed her gloves and pulled the roast beef from the oven. She set it on the countertop and placed the vanilla pudding inside. It was a delicious recipe she had stumbled upon by combining two others. The vanilla enveloped the entire kitchen with its strong aroma.

Virgil was studying the roast beef with interest. "You're sure this is not overdone?" he asked pointing to the dark crust covered in herbs.

"I can guarantee it's perfect. Well done on the outside, medium and juicy inside. I'll cover it with aluminum foil until you all come to the table."

"That's good then. I'll come, thank you. The tree is inside and set in its stand. You have only to tell me where you want it."

"You brought the tree. How lovely. We'll find a corner table somewhere." Lottie clapped her hands, happy that her boys will have a proper Christmas tree after all.

"Why do you need a table?" Virgil asked rushing after her into the living room.

Lottie stopped speechless. She'd assumed Virgil would bring a small pine tree to adorn the room. What she got was a huge, nine foot Majestic Douglas fir.

"If you don't like it, I could chop it down in size," Virgil assured her, anxious to please.

"No, no. It would be a pity."

The room was large with tall cathedral ceilings. It could accommodate the tall tree. In the end, they placed it in the bow window and Virgil adjusted it in the stand that it fit perfectly. They stepped back to admire their work.

"It's splendid," Lottie whispered.

Virgil nodded satisfied. "That, it is. I hope you don't have one of those tall toppers or it won't fit."

"No. It's an angel Wyatt bought for me the year we were married. I'll tie it in front of the top."

"The Gormans have some decorations also, but no one bothered to take them out in years."

"Doesn't Brianna like to decorate?" Lottie asked with curiosity, trying to understand better Tom's sister.

Virgil looked down studying the intricate pattern

in the western rug covering the hardwood floors. "Miss Brianna is special. She can ride as well as any cowboy and does any work necessary on the ranch. She is not into decorating and such. I heard she was different a few years back, but she changed. She also tried to please her father and despite her hard work and competence, she never succeeded."

"How sad!" Lottie understood disapproval very well. She had plenty in her life.

The smell of vanilla wafted from the kitchen and Lottie ran back. "My pudding."

Virgil wandered after her hoping to pinch a cookie. A wave of garlic aroma met him from a bowl on the counter. "Is this for the roast?" He asked bending his head to inhale it better.

"No. It's for the roasted vegetables," Lottie answered distracted. The pudding was just a tad over-caramelized on top. A dollop of whip cream should fix it. "Please call everyone in to have dinner."

She didn't finish talking when the door burst open and her two boys came in jumping and twirling and talking at the same time, barely able to contain their eagerness to tell her of their adventures on the ranch. They rode on a horse called Willow with Tom, and went on the range with a special wagon to spread extra feed to the cattle if it might snow tonight, and they saw an angry bull in a pen and some goats. Lottie was not sure how she felt about all this. She thought they would play on the ranch to consume the extra energy and that was great. However, the thought that her precious little boys were right in the middle of dangerous animals, was frankly scary.

"And the baby goat was so cute," Billy was saying. "Could we adopt her Mama? We could take her with us in our new house."

A baby goat? They were supposed to downsize, not increase their household with all the orphan animals the boys could find here. Even their previous large house wouldn't have been big enough to house them all.

"Ah, by the amazing aromas all over the house I think my brother hit the jackpot this time." The quiet brother Chris was rubbing his hands and Lottie smiled at him.

After him, Brianna came in, not in a much improved mood. Seeing all the bounty of food on the table, she just hmm-ed and took a seat near Billy who gave her a charming grin. She flicked his nose and rearranged the pillow under him so that he could comfortably reach the table.

Tom, freshly showered and changed, stopped in the doorway, stunned by the assortment of plates with food on the table. He frowned and absently took his place at the head of the table.

And just like that Lottie's happiness diminished considerably. Did she misunderstand him when he said she could do what she thought necessary to bring the family together? Was he angry because she presumed to take over his kitchen? She stood there looking at him with anxiety.

The door opened and Virgil followed by two other cowboys stopped there shyly, not sure of their welcome. It was obvious they made an effort to wash and change into clean clothes.

After a day of hard work they deserved a good meal, Lottie thought. She would deal with Tom later. She smiled at them warmly. "Please come in. I'm Lottie Donovan and I'll stay here at the ranch for a while until I find a new house for me and my boys. I know Virgil, who was so nice to bring a Christmas tree for us." She looked expectantly at the other two.

"This is Angel," Virgil said pointing at a giant of a man, with dark hair and dark beard. Near him, Virgil, who was a big man himself, looked dwarfed. "And this is our foreman, Hank. His wife Rachel went to see her family in Kansas."

"Nice to meet you all. Please come in and take a seat. Let's join hands and say Grace."

To say the meal was a success was an understatement. The plates were piled high with succulent roast beef and vegetables redolent of garlic. The pan of cornbread emptied fast. Lottie, who was afraid she had made Tom mad by cooking too much, now wondered if perhaps the food would not be enough. The cowboys attacked the food con gusto and moans of pleasure could be heard from time to time.

"I haven't tasted meat so tender and food so good in a long time, I don't mind telling you, ma'am. If I were not married, I'd ask you on the spot," Hank said leaning back in his chair, his hands on his stomach.

"But you are married and Rachel will tan your hide when she comes back if you so much as blink toward another woman," Virgil added his two cents.

"I ain't married. A woman who knows her way around a kitchen is worth her weight in gold. Especially one so pretty as Miss Lottie here," Angel, the giant, made his observation, chewing on a last piece of cornbread.

Tom's somber mood increased. "Temper your fervor, boys. Lottie here was not hired to cook for a whole bunch of unruly cowboys. She is an invited guest."

"But I don't mind cooking. On the contrary, it gives me tremendous pleasure to cook and have my food appreciated." Why was he upset? "If I overstepped your hospitality I'm sorry."

Tom covered her hand with his own larger one. "Lottie, first I want to thank you for preparing this dinner. No one on this ranch knows to cook worth a darn, pardon me, Hank, but Rachel is only slightly a better cook than any of us." He turned back to Lottie. "When I invited you here I hoped that from time to time, perhaps you'll bake us some of those incredibly good cupcakes. The green one was delicious; I don't know what you made it from."

"Vanilla and pistachios," Lottie answered smiling.

"The strawberry one was also a dream…"

"Forget the strawberry one, Boss," Virgil interrupted impatient. "Just tell her she can do whatever she wants in the kitchen, because none of us can. And let's eat the desert. That apple pie is so tempting and the vanilla smell …"

"Ah, homemade apple pie," Angel sighed looking longingly toward the source of the tempting smell.

It was more than Lottie could resist. A man wishing to taste her cooking. She brought the desert to the table. Silently, Chris gathered the dirty plates and mouthed, "No desert for me, thanks." He proceeded to clean the plates and load the dishwasher.

The desert was very much appreciated and the cowboys were not shy to shower Lottie with compliments. The only one who remained silent throughout dinner was Brianna, but she cut Billy's meat and helped him feed himself.

"Lottie," Tom said pushing his empty desert plate. "What I want to say is, I appreciate all you did, but you don't have to." He silenced the murmurs of protest. "You are my guest."

"But do I have your agreement to do what I consider important for all of us to have a nice Christmas celebration?" she asked. He nodded so she continued, "Then let me tell you my plans. Decorating is fun, but we are already late so I'll do it myself with the boys. Then, there are two major events till Christmas. One is the traditional Christmas pageant and concert in the Auditorium at the high school. And I'd like all of you to come. You'll have fun and I know it sounds magic, but you'll feel better afterwards."

The concert where Faith sung? No way was Tom

going to go. Like guessing his thoughts, Lottie touched him and whispered, "It's time."

"Time?" someone echoed.

"The right time," Lottie answered. "Then, this weekend was supposed to be a big birthday bash for Old Man Maitland. His seventieth birthday. Little Elliott came down with a cold so it will be postponed another week."

"We don't socialize with the Maitlands," Brianna said curtly, somewhat unhappy that this intruder took over her family life and she was determined to resist.

"I'm aware of that and this is the best moment to set aside old grudges and resentment and admit that the Maitlands are good neighbors."

"There are no grudges. It's just that we are not comfortable in large gatherings," Tom explained. It was the truth, he told himself. He was not resentful at all. He was a busy man and silly parties were not his favorite past times.

"Nonsense. I've known you since high school, Tom. You used to be such a great dancer."

"I've changed since high school, Lottie. That starry-eyed young man is no more. I'm a different man, with a ranch to run and a lot of responsibilities."

"It will do you good to forget about them for half a day," Lottie replied undaunted. It was then that Tom realized that the timid, smiling, complacent face Lottie presented to the world hid a firm, decided woman.

CHAPTER 7

When she was a little girl Lottie dreamed of having a decorated Christmas tree, with sparkly ornaments and lights. It never happened, as the people who fostered orphan children had no extra money for celebrating Christmas. At eighteen and for the first time on her own, Lottie bought a tiny, barely two foot tall tree and placed it on the table in the dorm she shared with two other students. She decorated it with stringed popcorn and paper homemade stars. It was the most beautiful thing she owned and it warmed her heart looking at it.

Later, married to Wyatt and after the boys were born, they had a big tree for Christmas and to the children's delight, they used to decorate it together, singing carols along with the radio and drinking hot chocolate. Every year she added to her collection of glass ornaments a few more precious pieces.

They would resurrect those happy times together in a new house, even if Wyatt was no longer with them.

Until then, Lottie was determined to make the best of this year for her little family and for the Gormans as well.

The angel was tied to the tip of the huge tree and humming to herself, Lottie was taking her time to choose the right ornament for the best spot on the tree, encouraged by Billy who was running around after his puppy. Early in the morning, Wyatt had looked regretfully one more time at the tree waiting for adornments and left with the cowboys to the barn to assist Tom in doctoring an injured calf.

"Mama, who invented the Christmas tree?" Billy asked, ever so practical.

"It was not invented, Billy. It was a tradition originated in Germany. And because it's a beautiful one and brings joy in our hearts, we adopted it as a nice way to celebrate Christmas."

The door opened and Brianna walked in, muttering to herself, "It's so cold, my breath froze in my lungs. It didn't snow last night but today it will for sure…"

"And we'll go out and make a snowman and play

in the snow," Billy laughed with joy at this idea.

Lottie smiled and filled a mug with hot chocolate and handed it to Brianna. While her eldest son, Wyatt had attached himself to Tom, following him everywhere, Billy preferred Brianna's company, who was equally friendly with him.

Brianna tickled the tummy of the puppy rolling on the floor and accepted Lottie's offering of the hot mug nodding her thanks. She looked at the tall fir tree set in front of the window, already adorned with strings of multicolored and white lights. As a decorator, Lottie was not into elegant and simple. She preferred to hang all her treasured ornaments, including her old paper stars.

"It's not exactly classy, but it has character," Brianna observed. "Dad didn't want to have a Christmas tree because he said it reminded him of Mama. After he died we followed the same pattern." She shrugged. "Or maybe we are too busy to bother."

"There is nothing wrong with remembering your loved ones. I wouldn't want my boys to forget Wyatt."

"Some memories, even nice ones are too painful

to remember. So we push them to the back of our mind." Brianna blinked, like being sorry for speaking so openly, and took a sip of the fragrant hot chocolate. "But you are mistaken if you think this," and she looked at the tree, "...or the good food will make Tom more amenable to go to your Christmas concert at school. Nothing in the world would convince him to attend a show directed by Faith Parker." The belligerent tone was back. Challenging.

"Listen Brianna. Tom, Faith, and I were classmates in high school. Tom and Faith were sweethearts. Both incredibly good-looking and high achievers. Tom as a football player. Faith singing like a nightingale. At the time everybody thought they were in love. They made a great couple together. Now I wonder, were they a couple because it was expected of them? I don't know."

"Tom has an honest heart. He'd have never courted Faith if he didn't love her," Brianna interrupted Lottie, defending her brother.

"It's true. Although Tom, as hero quarterback,

was expected to have the most spectacular girlfriend in high school. And that was Faith. I'm not saying he didn't love her. But think if Tom had chosen ….me as his girlfriend. I was a short, overweight teenager, a dork with my nose in a book all the time. Certainly I was not considered 'cool'. Not only I couldn't have been his girlfriend, but neither Tom nor Faith remembered me from high school."

"You said you're Faith's friend," Brianna remembered.

"Yes, I am now. We are both teachers at junior high and we get along pretty well."

"Frankly, I'm surprised. Faith is too overbearing and snotty to have a friend. I was shocked when I heard that she married Raul Maitland. She used to disparage him all the time. Unless she placed her interest before her prejudices, him being now such a wealthy rancher. But then so was Tom, if it was money she wanted."

Lottie smiled. "She's changed. A lot. And she loves Raul very much. They are a couple very much in love and Little Elliott is adorable. You'll see them when we'll go to Old Man Maitland's birthday bash."

"Another social event where Tom will be absent."

"He'll come to both events. It's time for Tom to return to social life. To laugh with his neighbors, to dance, and yes, to find the right woman for him and get married. It won't be me of course, but he needs to have a wife and children, to have a family to give meaning to his life."

Brianna was quite skeptical. "Tom can be very stubborn. He might not be as malleable as you think."

"Tom wants something he doesn't know how to achieve."

"What's that?"

"He wants his family to be happy. You and Chris."

Brianna snorted in disbelief. "Happiness is a chimera. Nobody can be truly happy. What nonsense. Did you promise him to bring happiness here?"

Lottie sighed. It was difficult to explain and she wondered if it was a mistake to talk openly to Brianna. "Tom feels that the way things are now can't continue.

And he is willing to try another way. My way. Do I have a recipe for happiness? Of course not. But I know people can be miserable and I want to bring this family together, instead of each one hiding in his turtle shell."

"And you think a concert where Faith will sing and be a star is the key to Tom's happiness?" Brianna asked disparagingly.

"Faith will be a star and just hearing her sing is a treat and a privilege. But being together and singing together celebrating Christmas will make us all feel better. The Auditorium will be packed for this concert."

There was a knock on the door and Virgil came in carrying a red poinsettia pot and some parcels. "Ms. Lottie, here are the things you wanted from town." He saw Brianna on the couch. "Pardon, Miss Brianna I thought you rode on the range with Hank and Angel." He placed his parcels down and taking his hat off, he twisted it in his hands, looking down and not knowing what to say. The tough cowboy blushed like a schoolboy.

What do you know, he's in love with her – Lottie thought.

Brianna was not impressed. She leaned back and said curtly, "As you can see I'm not on the range. You were wrong."

The moment became uncomfortable and Lottie jumped up from the chair. "Where are my manners? Virgil, here are some cookies and a mug of hot chocolate. I know you cowboys prefer coffee, but this is hot and it will warm you up."

"Thank you, ma'am. The cookies are divine."

She smiled at him approvingly like she did at any person who enjoyed her cooking. "We'll eat soon. How do you like our Christmas tree? It's not ready yet, but it looks better with the bright lights on."

He gulped the hot drink and paused to look at the tree. "It's very festive. You were right. It will make us feel better." He placed his empty plate and mug on the table nearby and straightened. "I have to go back to the barn. Thank you for the treat. Look, the mite fell asleep on the couch near Miss Brianna. Do you want me to carry him to his bed?"

Brianna answered before Lottie could. "It's not

necessary, Virgil. I'll take him. I'm sure you're needed in the barn."

He looked at her and nodded. Then he placed his Stetson on his head and turned to go.

"Don't forget we dine soon, Virgil. Tell the others to be ready." Lottie said after him.

He smiled sadly at her and nodded again. Then he left.

"Brianna, how could you be so impolite to him? He's a nice, hard-working man. He deserves better." Lottie was upset to see the gentle giant so rebuffed.

"Oh, he annoys me. He makes calf eyes at me and tramples over his own feet."

"He's sweet on you."

"I don't need him to be sweet on me. It's ridiculous," Brianna argued.

"Brianna, if you don't like him, I understand. You don't have to return his feelings. But he is a decent man, who went through a lot in life and made his own way without help since he was twelve years old."

"How do you know this?"

"I know because he told me. And I understand what he went through because I was in a similar situation myself. Not identical, I was in foster care, and he ran away from home, but I know what it means to be a child and to have no one in the world to care about you. So, please treat him politely."

"He is also driving all of us crazy with his curiosity. He pokes his nose in everyone's business."

Lottie rose and tried to lift Billy in her arms. The sleeping child was quite heavy. "He is harmless. Now please help me take Billy to bed."

CHAPTER 8

It was late in the afternoon and the sky was a darker grey, warning of another round of fresh snow soon to fall over the old frozen layer already covering the ground. Tom was cold and happy to be done checking his cattle spread throughout the east pasture. They were all snug and huddled together, with a good supply of feed. They should be fine until this coming blizzard would end.

Was he advancing in age that he felt tired to the bone? – Tom wondered. He was only thirty-two, he shouldn't feel like this. Ten years ago he had worked from dawn till dusk and had been still active at dinnertime. Now all he could think about was a hot shower and a good meal, and one of Lottie's cupcakes. She promised to make some today. And at lunch he smelled a savory stew, rich in soft beef and vegetables, with lots of herbs and spices. Just thinking of it, his mouth watered. And maybe he'd pilfer a cupcake before going to shower and change.

A man needed some sustenance to be able to work a whole day on the range. Bringing Lottie and her boys here had been a stroke of genius.

He was close to the barn when Angel who was inspecting the fence and pasture in the west came back galloping. Tom stopped the young gelding he was riding these days to spare old Willow. His horse was spirited but understood Tom's commands.

Anticipating trouble Tom turned to Angel who was breathing as hard as his black stallion.

"Boss, there are footprints in the snow to the west of here that have no business being there. I talked to Parker's boys and it was not them. Could have been someone from Maitland's ranch, but I doubt it."

"Where?"

"At the end of the west pasture where the Outlaw's Rocks are. The footprints disappeared into the Dead Indian's Canyon."

Yes, that smelled like trouble, Tom thought. There was no way to postpone seeing what was going on until the next day. The blizzard would wipe the tracks out. Sighing with regret, Tom chased out of his mind the image of a steaming bowl with fragrant stew and a plate with pink cupcakes nearby, and turned to Angel.

"Change the horse, take some blankets and flashlights, let Hank or Virgil know I'm headed to the Outlaw's Rocks and come after me. It will be dark soon so let's make it fast. Good thing that it's not snowing yet."

His gelding was probably tired after a day's work, but he was young and was not exhausted by a hard ride like Angel's horse. He was a good, reliable horse. Tom patted his neck to encourage him and urged him to a fast trot.

The Outlaw's Rocks were a strange rock formation that the wind had sculpted in millions of years and the rock on top resembled a human face, like the profile of a sphinx seen from a distance. The name however came from the late 1800s when an outlaw escaped from jail and hid there. An Indian scout who came with the posse after him was found shot dead in the nearby narrow canyon.

FOOTPRINTS IN THE SNOW

They said that the spirit of the Indian sought revenge and haunted the outlaw because when the posse found him after several days, he was running barefooted in the snow, mumbling to himself. They said he was driven to madness by the spirit of the man he shot.

It was one of the interesting bits of local folklore and when Tom related it to Old Man Maitland, he liked it so much that he included it in the book he was writing about the history of this part of southeastern Wyoming. 'There is always a kernel of truth in all these embellished stories and legends. That's why they are interesting,' he used to say. Old Man Maitland had Scottish and Indian Lakota blood in him and was very proud of his mixed heritage.

The wind picked up and rare snowflakes were swirling through the air. Tom was chilled to the bone. He wouldn't be surprised if he got a cold. He cursed whoever decided to take a hike on his land. Couldn't the intruder choose a warmer time?

After a twenty minutes ride, which seemed much

longer to a frozen Tom, he reached the outcrop of rocks called the Outlaw's Rocks. The sphinx like profile was spectacular, but Tom was in no mood to admire this corner of his ranch that had always fascinated him ever since he was a boy and his father brought him here. He had to bring Wyatt here, he thought. Wyatt was like him. Interested in the land and ranching. Billy, not so much. Perhaps when he'd be older. Billy preferred the company of Brianna and Chris. He loved riding with Chris in a slow gait listening what Chris was telling him about animals.

Tom stopped, his rifle ready. This time of year, hungry mountain lions came closer to the ranch hoping to snatch a lost calf. These were nature's laws of survival. Cougars were predators and Tom had to be prepared for unexpected attacks.

It was still light but barely and getting darker by the minute. Tom listened, but he could hear no noise except the wind. He took out his flashlight and pointed it in front of him. First he saw nothing but the day's old frozen layer of snow. Nothing. His horse was waiting obediently. Only his ears twitched from time to time but he gave no sign of sensing a human or animal presence nearby. Tom pushed his horse forward, thinking he'd come on a fool's errand when, in the focused beam of light he saw them clearly. Footprints in the snow.

Tom dismounted to study them better. Western boot, with metal reinforcements at the front and at the heel. Any ranch hand could wear boots like this, yet something was nagging at the edge of his mind that made this boot different. Hmmm!

Hoofbeats thundered in the distance and Tom readied his rifle. Then breathed easier. It was Angel on the same black stallion.

"Angel, you'll kill that horse. Why didn't you ask Hank for a different one?"

"Nah! Devil here has seven lives, and he loves excitement."

Devil was Angel's horse so if he wanted to ride him to exhaustion, he could. Angel laughed and patted the horse who neighed in response. "You see, he agrees. By the way, the little lady was worried about you and sent you this to tide you over." Angel reached behind him and gave him a thermos flask with hot coffee and a slightly squished package.

Eagerly, Tom took a large swig of coffee and closed his eyes with pleasure, feeling the heat penetrate his chilled bones. He opened the package and there were two cupcakes. One pink and one green. Ah, Lottie, how thoughtful of you! He gave the pink one to Angel. "Here, the pink one is strawberry flavored."

"No need Boss," Angel refused laughing. "The pink one is for you. I had chocolate iced ones at home."

Tom gulped down the cupcakes, washed them with more coffee and they went to look at the prints. Angel climbed behind the rocks to search and Tom looked toward the canyon. The walls of the narrow canyon were steep and the footprints ended there like someone took the next step into the air. Tom was at the edge of the canyon pointing his flashlight downwards. It looked like there was some dark colored spot there, but the steep incline and narrow space didn't allow for a better look. Maybe in plain daylight they could go down and explore.

Angel called to him. "Boss, come quick."

When Tom reached Angel, up among the big boulders, he saw hidden in a natural stone shelter a small, old tent.

"Who would set house here among the rocks on my land?" Tom asked.

Angel pointed to a makeshift fire pit, an old skillet abandoned nearby, a coffeepot and what looked like a pair of dirty, maybe with traces of dried blood, woolen socks.

"Shall I gather all this, Boss," Angel asked.

"No, no. They are dirty. Leave them here. I'll call the sheriff tomorrow and let him know." Tom sneezed and shivered. "If I get a cold because of this trespasser, he will be sorry, regardless of his reason for living on my land. "I had enough. Let's go back. Maybe we'll send Virgil tomorrow to inspect the site. You know how curious he is." Tom mounted his gelding and barely nudged him and the horse was happy to trot in the direction of the ranch house and the stable.

By the time they arrived home, snow was falling in earnest and Tom was shivering seriously, coughing and sneezing. The sight of his ranch house all lighted up and the Christmas tree in the window visible from afar, warmed his heart. Lottie opened the front door and ran to him. With frozen hands Tom caught the pommel and dismounted.

"Tom, it's so late and it was getting dark. Virgil wanted to ride after you two."

He opened his arms and she nestled close to him. He buried his face in her soft, curly hair.

Virgil came from the barn and took his horse's bridle. "I'll take care of him, Boss. Go inside. Angel said you were coughing and sneezing," he said alerting Lottie.

She touched his cheek, which was frozen, then she placed her hand inside his coat and shirt where he was hot. She shook her head. "I don't like it. You might catch a cold." She took him by the hand inside the warm house where a fire was roaring in the fireplace. She ran a hot bath for him and sent Chris to help him with his bath. Like he was a small kid who needed help. He was coughing and sneezing so hard he had tears in his eyes and Chris stuck a box of tissues in his hand.

In the end he chased everybody out and sunk in the hot water with a moan of pleasure. Usually Tom was a shower man. Fast in, lather, rinse and out. He had no time to waste in the tub. Brianna enjoyed it and her bathroom always smelled of all sorts of exotic bath salts and foams.

A brief knock on the door woke him up. He'd fallen asleep in the tub, the water was tepid now and his skin looked like a prune.

"Tom, I'm coming in," Chris warned him before entering. "Lottie was worried you might be sick. She sent me to help you out and to dress." He smirked at Tom.

"I'm fine," Tom muttered, then looked straight at Chris repeating, "I'm fine, I'll be ready in five minutes." Sometimes he forgot Chris couldn't hear well. His newly found brother worked and lived like any other person, and they didn't remember always to look at him when talking so he could read lips.

In the kitchen, the table was set only for him; the

others, including Angel had finished eating. Lottie was hovering nearby, straightening his napkin and pushing the bread basket closer.

"I don't want to be a bother, Lottie," he said caressing her cheek, marveling at how soft and unblemished her skin was. "But I thank you for waiting for me."

"Of course, how could I not, Tom? Here the stew is warm. I heated it again when I heard you coming."

The stew was just like in his dreams, fragrant of herbs and spices. He took his spoon and tasted. Mmm! Delicious. The meat was soft and the vegetables also but without being mushy. Tom broke a chunk of the fresh bread. It smelled of garlic and it had some herbs in it.

"Rosemary and garlic bread," Lottie told him smiling at his obvious enjoyment of her food.

"I love it," Tom said and raising his napkin to his face sneezed mightily. And again. "I hope I didn't catch a cold."

"I think you did. Tomorrow I'll make chicken soup for you and you'll take a break for a day and stay home. Chris and the men can manage one day without you."

He opened his mouth to argue, but looked into Lottie's concerned hazel eyes and nodded. He had to report the trespasser to the sheriff and check on how the animals fared after tonight's snowfall. Staying at home he'd be bored to death. But it was nice to have a person genuinely worried about him and to be spoiled with good food. Brianna cared about him, but a pat on the back and 'you'll be fine' was all she offered.

CHAPTER 9

The next day Tom's cold vanished. No more sneezing or coughing. He was ready to ride and inspect how his cattle had survived the snowfall.

After he polished clean his plate with eggs and sausages, he pulled the plate with cupcakes closer and carefully picked a white frosted one with multi-colored sprinkles on it. He bit in it and savored the taste. Vanilla, a hint of almond and was it rum? It was divine.

"I'm glad you like it," Lottie said from the other side of the table where she was grading some papers.

"Sorry, I was lost in thought." Tom answered, although if he were to say what was the subject of such profound thinking, what could he say? That he was comparing white frosting with pink on a cupcake? His eyes stopped on her papers. "Math? You are a math teacher?"

Lottie smiled, her warm, sincere smile that went straight to a person's heart. "Yes, I'm a math teacher. I always liked the exact quality of numbers. There is only one correct answer. No two ways about it. Straightforward. I am good at it."

"I thought women were more into poetry."

"Not all women. If you knew Ms. Proffitt, our principal and our ex-math teacher you'd agree. Actually you should remember her."

Tom grimaced. "Not the Terror Proffitt. She is your principal?"

"Yep. Still unmarried and strong-willed. She is a force to reckon with. But I think she likes us, Faith and me." Oops, taboo subject, Faith Parker. "Sorry," she mumbled.

Tom stood up wincing a bit at the pain in his muscles after the record work day he put in the day before. "Come here, Lottie. You don't have to say sorry, when you did nothing wrong and we should be able to talk openly about Faith. Don't you think so?" He pulled her to him wanting to erase the worry in her hazel eyes. She caught her lower lip between her teeth and Tom's eyes went right there, attracted like a magnet by her plump rosy lips, her very kissable lips. Every reasonable thought in his mind went away, except the desire to taste Lottie's lips which looked even more tempting than the icing on her cupcakes. Tom bent his head and captured her lower lip and gently sucked on it. He pulled her closer still and raised one hand to steady her head so he could taste her lips better and give her the full-blown kiss that frankly he wanted for a while now. She made a humming noise, of agreement, he thought, and she circled his waist with her arms to get as close to him as possible. She was short but fit him perfectly, all soft and womanly curves. His body responded promptly, reminding him that there were needs he'd ignored for too long.

He buried his hand in her soft hair and deepened the kiss. Urgently, he pushed her against the table, ready to lift her up, when the grading papers and some books fell on the floor.

"Oh," she said looking down and realizing where they were. Her hands were on his chest after undoing the first buttons of his shirt. "You're hot," she said the first thing that crossed her mind. And promptly blushed.

"I'm still hot, yes. I don't know what came over me," he added although he knew very well. For whatever reason he was attracted to Lottie Donovan and he wanted her like he had never wanted another woman before, including the beautiful Faith Parker. His body had decided it was Lottie he wanted and no other. The first time he'd felt this attraction he thought it was a fluke, surely not short Lottie, cute as she was. Now he had to acknowledge that it had been no fluke. He was very attracted to her. And it was too bad because she was a guest in his house, a vulnerable widow still missing her husband. What kind of man took advantage of her in such a situation? He liked to believe he had the decency to keep his hands off her, even if his body disagreed.

Her look was uncertain and vulnerable and slowly her hands let go of his shirt buttons. With regret he watched her step back.

"I guess we shouldn't," he muttered. "Not in the kitchen," he added, leaving open the idea that he would like to continue where they left it, in a more private place.

Right then, the door opened and Chris came in. "What?" he asked.

"Lottie had dropped her papers and I was helping her pick them up," Tom said scooping up the papers on the floor.

"Why is your shirt open to your waist?"

"I was hot. Remember, I have fever," Tom answered annoyed at his brother. What was this? Twenty questions? He had a few of his own that his dear brother hasn't answered in all the years he lived with them.

"Yes. And he was taking two aspirins," Lottie added and took this opportunity to make him swallow two pills before letting him go outside. Tom was notoriously against taking medicine when not necessary. And he didn't consider a sneeze a situation that required medicine.

What Lottie didn't tell Tom was that yesterday when classes were over she found another piece of paper in the windshield of her car, written in black marker:

'You can't escape'. And this time she knew it was not a prank of the neighbor's kids. It was a psycho, who wanted to scare her. Why her? One of her foster parents used to joke when a person was nasty, 'he is envious of my poverty', he used to say.

She remembered this now because it made no sense why someone would want to harm her. Fearing for her boys, she went to see TJ Lomax and showed him the paper. She found also the first one she had received. It was in her car, wrinkled.

"Do you know of any person, adult or child – children can be malicious too – with whom you had a conflict or just words in contradiction recently?" TJ asked peering at her above his reading glasses. "Any kid you gave a bad grade and he protested."

"No kid, no. No one really," Lottie hesitated. "Well, do you remember, Doug Williams, from my last foster care home?"

"Doug, the bully. Of course I remember." TJ didn't add that not only did he remember Doug, but he also had a small scar on his hand from the time when he caught Doug pulling Lottie's blond curls and he twisted Doug's arm. When he let go of him, warning him to stay away from Lottie, Doug pulled a knife from his pocket and grazed TJ's hand. He had a mean streak and TJ wouldn't be surprised if Doug ended up in jail. He had to check on that.

He made annotations on his tablet while Lottie told him about the surprise encounter with Doug in front of the school. TJ laughed when he heard how Faith had chased Doug away. "That Faith Parker is quite something," he said with undisguised admiration.

"Yes, she is," Lottie admitted. "Faith is beautiful, smart, talented, and brave. How can anyone compete with such perfection?" She sighed.

TJ took off his glasses and studied her with attention. "Are you in love with Raul Maitland, Lottie?"

Lottie looked at him stunned. "With Raul? Good Lord, of course not. What gave you that idea?"

TJ breathed easier. Lottie in love with Raul would have been heartbreak in the making for her. "The way you said it. Like you wanted to compete with Faith and realized it was hopeless."

"That's because of course I can't compete with Faith. From high school she was the most beautiful, talented…"

"In high school Faith was all this and also spoiled and snotty. A brat."

"But she had the admiration of all the boys and she had the most perfect boyfriend, Tom Gorman. In fact, he is in love with her and he can't forget her even now."

"Ah, Tom Gorman." TJ placed his glasses back on. He must be getting senile if it took him so long to understand that Lottie's dream man was not Raul, but Tom Gorman. On one hand, TJ was relieved it was not a married man Lottie wanted. A happily married man like Raul Maitland. He trusted that his Lottie had better judgment. And he was happy that after almost two years of mourning her dead husband, Lottie was ready to live again. It would have been a pity otherwise as Lottie had so much love to give and deserved to be loved in return. Tom Gorman, Hmm! Not a bad choice. But first, "Listen to me, Lottie. Faith is a great woman, but men are different and they prefer a lot of other qualities in a woman. Don't sell yourself short, Lottie. You have a lot to offer to the right man. Your generous, loving heart is the most precious treasure you can offer to a man. As for Tom Gorman, he had Faith as his girlfriend for years and things didn't heat up. On the contrary, they cooled down. Trust me, my dear, Tom is not carrying a torch for Faith." He observed Lottie's face and the emotions that could be so easily read. Time to change the subject. He was not Dear Abby to give sentimental advice, or was he? "Now, tell me if you can think of other people you argued with recently."

"My sister-in-law, Alicia. She doesn't have children. I think she can't have children. She suggested that she could offer more to Wyatt and Billy than I can. She didn't go as far as to threaten to take them, but I think that is her plan. Do you think any judge would agree with her?" Lottie asked anxiously.

"No, of course not. You are the boys' mother and a teacher, which is a plus. You can give them a great education."

Lottie bit her lower lip. "I don't have even a fraction of the money she has and I know judges prefer married parents, and Alicia is married."

"You have a good job and enough money to insure a decent life for them. It's not your fault that your husband was killed in the line of duty. On the contrary, it might impress the judge. Come on, girl. Chin up."

Lottie nodded. "It helps that Alicia lives in Texas, and not here."

"I agree. I don't think she is the one leaving intimidating notes on your windshield." TJ hesitated before speaking. "I don't want to frighten you, but I think it's better to be warned. In an unrelated case of robbery, the police caught a man who acted as a driver. He spilled the beans in a plea deal with the prosecutor and said that the man who killed your husband is back in the area intent on revenging his brother's death and killing more policemen. That's all I know. But be careful and wary of any unknown man who crosses your way."

VIVIAN SINCLAIR

CHAPTER 10

It was the day of the Christmas pageant and concert at the high school, an event highly anticipated by the entire town. A lot of people had gathered to see their children performing on stage and to hear Faith and her choir singing carols. But most people had come to enjoy a nice evening with their neighbors and friends and to sing along with the children in the choir.

Tom Gorman, who was waiting for the right moment to make an excuse and stay home, saw with surprise that the sweet, mild-mannered Lottie became a true dynamo, who took them all by storm. First, she marched right to the bunkhouse and ordered the men to take a bath, don their best Sunday clothes, and be ready to drive to town for the concert. There were some grumbles of protest, squelched easily by the promise of a special dinner tonight crowned by Lottie's to-die-for vanilla and custard flaky pie. Just thinking about it made Tom's mouth water.

Then, Lottie took a deep breath and braced

herself for talking to Brianna. Good luck trying to bribe her with yummy food. Brianna liked well prepared meals better than burnt food. Who wouldn't? However, she appreciated Lottie's presence in the house not because of the gourmet food, but because it meant she did not have to cook herself or to do other domestic chores that were not her ideal past time.

"No, no, no. I'm not going to town," she said and stomped her foot to make her point. "I don't like primping and I haven't worn a dress for ages."

Keeping her smile, Lottie opened her closet to look inside. "Let's see." Brianna's closet had an assortment of jeans and mostly plaid shirts. Not very promising. It was true that most people came to the concert dressed in jeans. Laramie was a ranching town after all. Brianna could go wearing her best jeans and fit right in with everyone else. However, Lottie wanted to make this day special and dress up in a nice outfit.

At the back of the closet, she saw a dress covered in a black plastic bag. She lifted the plastic and saw a beautiful blue dress with a rip at the shoulder. She could sew it up in no time at all.

"No, not that one," Brianna barked from behind Lottie.

"Why not? It's so pretty."

After a brief hesitation, Brianna said, "Bad memories."

Lottie nodded. She understood and respected bad memories. She had some herself. And she also understood the need for privacy and didn't ask questions. Without another word, she placed the dress at the back of the closet. Brianna will have to face her demons eventually, but not today.

She picked a pair of newer, black jeans and came out of the closet. "Here. I have the right sweater that will go great with this."

Lottie knew right away what to give Brianna to wear. None of her dresses would fit her. Brianna was taller and had a slim, athletic body. Lottie chose her most precious sweater, which was made of lavender cashmere and had been received as a Christmas gift from Faith Parker two years ago. It was beautiful and expensive.

Lottie kept it for special occasions. She buried her face in its incredible softness, and then took it to Brianna.

"Here. This will complement your blue eyes."

It was a lovely color and Brianna accepted it, muttering grudgingly "Thank you."

Lottie hugged her despite Brianna's reluctance to return the hug. Lottie didn't mind. She understood that in this family each person lived like a turtle, in the same house with the others, but isolated in his own shell. Lottie had big hopes of coaxing them to come together as a family and to talk, really talk, sharing their burdens with each other. She had promised Tom.

Next, she went to find Chris. He was in the barn, oiling a saddle in the tack room and humming to himself.

Lottie positioned herself directly in front of him so he could read her lips. "Chris, I expect you to go to wash and put on your best jeans and shirt to attend the Christmas festivities at the school auditorium."

He shook his head. "Not going to happen, Ms. Lottie. Me at a concert? Why should I bother? I can't hear anything."

Lottie took a deep breath. "You can hear something with your hearing aids. Besides, the noise will be so loud that you will hear it for sure. Even if you don't, people will be singing together and not all are musically trained. Don't you see? It's not about hearing the music. It's about joining our friends to celebrate together Christmas by singing carols. You know carols, don't you?"

Reluctantly he nodded.

"It will be fun, you'll see. Go and get ready. We'll drive together," Lottie patted his arm and left.

She found Tom pacing the family room. He was not in a good mood.

"What's this I hear that you are bullying everyone to go to the pageant?" he asked her as soon as she came in.

"Tom, you gave me free hand to make this a family," Lottie started to speak.

"Going to the pageant is not going to make us a family. It's going to make us all miserable. Don't you understand? I certainly don't intend to go." He turned

113

and looked at the snowy landscape outside.

Lottie came closer and leaned against him. "Look, I understand you don't want to face Faith Parker, but it's been two years since she married Raul."

"Is that what you think? You are wrong. It's not Faith I don't want to face. It's all the blasted people who will avidly watch me coming face to face with Faith and Raul, expecting a show of some sort, maybe even a fight between Raul and me. It's them I want to avoid."

"Yes, human nature is inclined to gossip and enjoy other people's drama. But they are your neighbors and you have to face them."

"Not in public, I don't," he argued stubbornly.

"Tom, you were my hero in high school…"

"I was?" For some reason, this made him feel marginally better.

"Don't pretend you don't know. You were the hero of this entire town. Our best quarterback. All the girls were secretly in love with you."

"Including you, Lottie?" he asked her grinning.

"'Vanity thy name is… football player'," she

114

improvised her quote. "Yes, including me, but you gave all your attention to Faith. Look, years have gone by and we are older and smarter now. Faith is a wonderful person, who is very much in love with Raul, and she is my best friend. I don't want to tiptoe and bite my tongue every time I talk about her in this house. I think you should accept that life goes on and in order to prove this to yourself and to the others, you have to face the Maitlands publicly, naturally, like nothing is amiss. Don't forget we are going to the Old Man's birthday bash next week."

Tom groaned. "Why does every social event have to include the Maitlands?"

"Because this is a sparsely populated land and we have to socialize with our neighbors and to help each other if the necessity arises." She leaned again on his arm and a flowery fragrance with a hint of vanilla came to his nostrils. Her shampoo mixed with Lottie's personal smell. He buried his face in her curls inhaling. It drove him crazy. Crazy with lust.

Unaware, Lottie continued. "Listening to Faith

sing is such joy. She is so talented. You shouldn't deprive yourself of this pleasure, just because you resent her for marrying Raul. Let's enjoy the Christmas celebration without any resentment."

And so, they all went to the concert. The auditorium was packed and Tom was stopped by neighboring ranchers to talk about livestock, winter, and the price of beef. He knew most of these people. Lottie went to help behind the curtain, especially because Billy had an important part in the Nativity play; he was one of the sheep.

The Maitland brothers were there, all three of them and their family. Tom nodded politely from a distance. He said hello to TJ Lomax and saluted courteously the rather stiff female he was escorting. "Ma'am."

"Ah, you remember Ms. Proffitt?"

Terror Proffitt? This was his former math teacher who gave them all nightmares in high school. What was TJ doing in her company?

"I heard you offered temporary housing to Lottie

Donovan and her boys," Ms. Proffitt said looking at him with the same severe, spearing eyes. "You take good care of them, you hear? I'll be watching you," she threatened and nodding regally walked away to the first row. TJ waved his hand and rushed after her.

Then Lottie returned and the Nativity play began. It went well, without a glitch, except for the moment when Joseph said, "We'll sleep here in the stable with the sheep" and one of the sheep said dramatically, "Meeeh!" People applauded and because Joseph was startled by this unscripted interruption, the sheep encouraged by the success, said again, 'Meeeh!'

The second part of the pageant was musical. The choir started with Christmas carols and the audience clapped their hands and sang along. Then several students performed individually. Lottie was amazed that every year Faith discovered new talent to perform. For example, a young boy came on stage playing the harmonica and then called for his cousin visiting from West Virginia, who was a fiddler. They were a rousing success, and left the audience shouting for more.

Lottie was happy to see that not only were the gruff ranch hands having a good time, but also Brianna was tapping her booted foot and Chris was clapping his hands. She was sure the noise was loud enough for him to hear.

At the end, Faith and the choir came back on stage and when Faith started to sing, there was not a soul in the auditorium with dry eyes. Her voice was clear soprano and it touched every heart.

Tom was enthralled by her and looking at Faith he remembered exactly how much he had admired and loved her. Was he a glutton for punishment to torture himself by seeing Faith again? He felt Lottie's hand squeeze his in understanding. It had a calming effect, helping him look at the whole situation in a more detached way. He grabbed Lottie's hand and allowed the noise to envelop him. A beautiful woman with a splendid voice sang carols on the stage. He pulled Lottie closer and for the second time that day a familiar flowery fragrance with a hint of vanilla came to his nostrils. He inhaled and smiled into her worried eyes. He was fine.

And for good measure, while people around them clapped and sang at the top of their lungs and in perfect discordance, Tom brushed his lips against Lottie's tempting rosy ones.

CHAPTER 11

The concert ended and people still humming or laughing together started to leave the auditorium. Lottie went down at the stage level to wait for her boys. All went well until unavoidably they met with the Maitlands, waiting for Faith.

Lottie grabbed Tom's hand trying to hold him back. No such luck. He advanced until he was face to face with Raul Maitland. They looked at each other like two fighters in a ring.

Lottie had to intervene to avoid the disaster. "Raul, I think you're proud of Faith. Each year she delights us with a wonderful Christmas pageant. The concert this year was great. Isn't it, Tom?" she said, elbowing him.

"Hmm," he grumbled, keeping his eyes fixed on the other man.

True to his prediction, people had slowed their pace out, some stopped entirely, curious to see the meeting between Tom and Raul.

Faith and Lottie's two boys joined them.

"Mama, did you see how well I played the sheep?" Billy pulled at Lottie's hand. "Everybody applauded," he continued, jumping up and down.

"Yes, he is a budding artist," Faith confirmed laughing, unaware of the tension between the two men.

"Congratulations, Raul," Tom spat. It was not very clear what he was talking about - Faith's performance, Raul getting his girl...

"Where is Little Elliott tonight?" Lottie asked desperate for conversation.

"With his grandma at home. She loves him." Faith leaned on Raul who hooked a proprietary arm around her waist.

"It's good that you get along well," Lottie said, and then wanted to bit her tongue for introducing another thorny subject.

Faith laughed again. "We do, we get along famously since she understood I have no desire whatsoever to take her place in the kitchen."

Lottie smiled, although it was beyond her

understanding why Faith would not wish to prepare meals in her own house, for her family. This was what home and family was about, lovingly cooking favorite food for them. At least in Lottie's view. It seemed that Faith had other priorities and her Raul didn't mind.

"Now Tom, shake hands politely and let's go," Lottie instructed him, her attention caught by Brianna who was close to the exit, when a tall cowboy grabbed her arm. Lottie opened her mouth to tell Tom, not even aware that he was extending his hand to Raul. Their handshake was a signal to the onlookers that nothing exciting was going to happen and the audience started to move on. Only Faith saw that the handshake lasted too long and the two men were engaged in a contest of strength. Faith playfully slapped their hands making them separate and shook her finger at Raul.

Lottie looked again at Brianna who had freed her arm from the cowboy's grip and was exchanging heated words with him. He tried to grab her again when, coming between them, Virgil pushed the cowboy away. The cowboy assessed Virgil's size and strength, said some words scathingly and left. Virgil looked at Brianna with concern, but she waved her hand dismissively and walked out of the auditorium, leaving Virgil there alone.

"I hope to see you all next week at the Old Man's birthday party," Faith said ready to go.

"Of course, we'll be there," Lottie confirmed, just as Tom opened his mouth to refuse politely, but firmly.

"I don't think we…," he started but Lottie looked at him admonishingly, so he snapped his mouth shut. Darn, the woman was meddling. Didn't she understand that he had no intention of socializing with the Maitlands?

Later, when he was driving back to his ranch, he told Lottie, who was humming a Christmas song along with the car radio, "I am not planning to go to the Maitlands next week. I did as you asked and I came to town for this show. I even shook hands with Raul."

"You call that a handshake?"

"Yes, that's what it was. What would you call it?"

"A pissing contest between two mature adults,

who should know better," Lottie answered scoffing.

"That's because Raul wanted to prove he is stronger. Bah! I can take Raul any time if he wants an armwrestling contest."

"I'm sure you can, but there is not going to be any contest. You two will have to get along nicely like two civilized neighbors."

"Stop interfering," Tom told her, pushed to the limit. Although if he were honest, today's school performance had not been so bad. Talking to old friends had been pleasant, the music had been nice, and Faith had a splendid voice. And his cowboys had enjoyed the celebration. Working on a ranch was hard work. Now and again, when they went to town on a Saturday night to play cards and get drunk, could not be considered socializing or even fun. They all needed a distraction from their every day routine. Today was fun and exactly what they all needed.

He turned to Lottie to admit this. She had tears in her eyes and was blinking to chase them away. He stopped the truck on the side of the secondary road that led to his ranch. "I'm sorry, Lottie." He looked behind on the back seat where the two boys had fallen asleep, after chattering like magpies about their performances. "I didn't mean to upset you. You are a guest in my house."

She sniffed and smiled through her tears. "Every guest becomes unwelcome if she stays too long. I should be looking for a new house for us. It's just that I was busy with the Christmas preparations."

The idea that she might leave struck Tom like a thunderbolt. He didn't want to think about it because it was unthinkable. He told himself that it would be impossible to return to Brianna's burned steaks after being spoiled by Lottie's culinary delights. But he knew that what he would miss the most would be seeing Lottie's smiling face every morning and being peppered by the boys' questions about ranching.

"Look, you promised to stay with me until after the new year. And you can't uproot the boys before Christmas."

"I don't want to be in the way. After foster care, I swore I'd never live in a house where I'm merely tolerated, but unwanted," she whispered.

"Lottie, how can you think you are in the way in my house?" he bent to kiss her to explain in the only way he could that she was appreciated and wanted. Faith was right that he was not good with words. A noise from the children reminded him that they were not alone. "Later," he promised, caressing her cheek.

As soon as he stopped his truck in front of the house, Virgil came to talk to him. "Boss, when I came home I saw some strange lights in the bushes yonder, at a distance beyond the barn and, you know I have a curious nature…"

"We all know that, Virgil."

"Yes, well, I found footprints in the snow, beyond the outbuilding near the barn. They were fresh and they were not ours," he said scratching his head. "Do you want me to go to investigate?"

"Not now, Virgil. We're all going to the kitchen to enjoy the special dinner Lottie has prepared."

Virgil's eyes lit up. "Yes, I smelled brisket in the

slow cooker and the whole kitchen was enveloped in the vanilla aroma from the custard."

"You all come in and after dinner we'll talk in the barn. No word at the dinner table that might alarm the women." Tom turned to go when Virgil's next words stopped him.

"It could be the no-good cowboy who pestered Miss Brianna after the show."

"What cowboy?"

"I don't know. I haven't seen him before and I know all the boys at the neighboring ranches. Could be newly hired, although…"

"Although what?"

"He was alone. I mean everybody there had come with family or friends. He had no one with him." Virgil hesitated before speaking. "Miss Brianna seemed to know him." He shook his head. "I might be wrong."

"I'll talk to my sister."

"About the footprints. There was only one person. It was dark and I couldn't go farther to see if he came with a car or on horseback. That's why I wanted to investigate."

"Tomorrow in daylight. If he didn't harm the animals or steal anything while we were gone, then we'll be safe until tomorrow. Whoever he is, he's a stranger who didn't come to the front door to state his business. He came prowling when we were away. For what purpose, I don't know, but I'm sure it's nothing good. So we have to be cautious and prepare for a confrontation."

"Yes, Boss," Virgil said, perked up by the idea of a confrontation with a prowler.

"And Virgil, curiosity or not, don't do anything risky."

When they were all sitting around the table, Lottie brought the brisket and the pot roast with roasted vegetables to the table and while Tom carved the meat, she brought another steaming platter.

"Potatoes," Hank said hopeful.

"No, it's my mushroom risotto," Lottie corrected him.

"Mushroom risotto," Virgil echoed.

"What's a risotto?" Angel asked.

"She means rice," Virgil clarified dryly and not very enthusiastic.

"Hmm, rice…" Hank mumbled.

Only Chris was looking from one to the other smiling amused and taking the serving spoon heaped a large portion of rice next to his slices of brisket.

Hank, still muttering to himself, accepted some of the rice that Lottie placed on his plate. He tasted, gingerly at first; then a second forkful followed. "This is good," he admitted and without talking proceeded to eat and clean his plate.

"Ma'am, I apologize. I should have known that whatever you cooked will taste divinely." Virgil saluted.

"Don't be a clown, Virgil," Brianna cut him short. Lottie wondered if Brianna didn't like Lottie's cooking to be praised or if she had a habit of bullying Virgil who was sweet on her. Hard to say.

"Brianna, no insults at the dinner table," Tom addressed her rather curtly.

Brianna shrugged. Lottie hoped her famous

vanilla custard pie will sweeten them all, especially because she had a surprise second custard pie, this one caramel flavored. And indeed it did.

CHAPTER 12

"Watcha' doing, Tom? Is the cow sick?" a childish voice asked from behind the door.

Tom was sitting on a bale of hay in one of the stalls in the barn, watching carefully one of his pregnant heifers giving birth. It was not progressing well. The birth was breach and the animal was already tired. Tom was impatient for veterinarian Tristan Maitland to arrive.

Just then Hank looked inside the stall. "The vet is here."

Tom sighed relieved. Tristan would know what to do to save the mother and the calf. He came out of the stall to talk to him, but Tristan's attention was already focused on the expectant cow and he knelt near the struggling animal, running his hands up and down its swollen abdomen. "Breach," was all he said and prepared to help by turning the calf into position.

Knowing his animal was in good hands, Tom stepped outside. The air was cold and ominous dark clouds signaled the approaching snowfall.

"Will the cow die?" The two boys were looking at him with worried eyes. Since his father's death, little Billy was afraid of losing someone else in his life. He clutched his puppy to his thin chest. Tiger didn't try to escape because he was stuffed with good food from Lottie's kitchen, Tom thought, looking at the fat puppy sleeping in Billy's arms.

"No, she'll be fine. Soon she will have a newborn calf to take care of," Tom assured them, guiding them inside where it was warmer. He sat on another bale of hay and took the two of them on his knees. "Tristan is the best vet around these parts."

Wyatt nodded solemnly. "Yes, he is. Uncle TJ says so."

"You guys often go to his clinic with TJ," Tom observed, curious about the strange friendship between the friendly vet – he was friendly despite being a Maitland – and the surly, taciturn private investigator. It was also true that Tom couldn't imagine TJ acting as babysitter to the two little boys, who were not related to him, even if they called him 'uncle'.

"Yes, we do. 'Cause TJ's retriever Goldie is getting old and she needs Tristan to check her health often," Billy explained. "We like it there. There are a lot of nice animals. We even saw a parrot once. He said swear words and Uncle TJ didn't let us listen to him very long." Billy sighed and looked at his older brother, who nodded in a tacit agreement.

Tom envied the easy way the two boys communicated and he wondered whether his childhood would have been different if he'd had a brother to share all the mischievous things boys do at this age. A partner in crime – so to speak. Well, he had a brother now and it was pointless to regret what might have been. Was his old man at fault for having an affair and treating it carelessly? Maybe. Tom wanted to be closer to his brother, but talking was not his forte and Chris used his deafness as a shield to keep them all at a distance. How could Tom make him understand that he was welcome in the Gorman family? Tom wished that Chris were his friend, like the Maitland brothers, Raul and Lance, were.

Deep in thought, he didn't notice that the two

boys were again communicating without words.

"Uh, Tom…," Wyatt started to speak.

Tom looked from one mischievous face to the other. "What have you two little …angels done now?"

"We haven't done anything," Billy jumped to deny.

"…Not anything wrong," Wyatt filled in. The dog woke up and squirmed in Billy's arms to be let loose. Once on the floor, he went to explore the surroundings. "You see," Wyatt continued. "…it's close to Christmas and we wanted to give Mama a gift. We have some money, almost three dollars, but we're not sure it'll be enough. Then this morning we found a piece of jewelry. We know that Brianna doesn't wear jewelry. I don't think the cowboys wear either, but could you ask them, because if they don't, we thought…"

"Hoa, stop right there. You two have found a piece of jewelry this morning. On this ranch." Tom repeated the words to be sure he'd heard right. Wyatt nodded solemnly. "Where?"

"There." Billy pointed outside. "Behind that

brush, close to the barn."

"You see, this morning, we followed Virgil, who walked beyond the barn, holding the bridle of his horse. He looked around on the ground, but probably he didn't find what he was looking for and he mounted and rode away," Wyatt supplied the explanation.

"He didn't see you?" Tom asked. Virgil was curious, but no matter how caught up in his search, he wouldn't have abandoned the boys without leaving them in someone's care.

"Nah, he was upset 'cause Brianna had rebuffed him again this morning. Why do you s'ppose she doesn't like him? Virgil is the best looking cowboy I know," Wyatt said. "Well, except for you, Tom," he amended.

Virgil, with his homely face could hardly be called good-looking, and in any case not 'the best'. But the boys liked him – Tom thought.

"Mama says that some people don't like you, no matter what you do. You can't please them. Do your best and go forward," Wyatt observed philosophically.

Billy frowned. "He can't. Virgil is in love with

her."

This was news to Tom. "Who is in love?"

"Duh, Virgil is in love with Brianna. Everyone on the ranch knows," Billy said.

Everyone, but Tom. How did this happen without him noticing? Was he so preoccupied by his own problems that a kid who had just arrived here, had to enlighten him in the more subtle goings on at the ranch?

"And he can't go on with his life if she keeps rejecting him. It must be hurtful. Have you ever been in love Tom?" Billy asked him.

"Once. Or so I thought. That I was in love and that she returned my feelings." He must be melancholy to share personal feelings with a five year old boy. Yet he continued. "I was wrong. She didn't love me and married another."

Wyatt nodded with understanding. "She didn't think you were good looking enough for her?"

"Probably that too. She said I was dull and boring."

"How could that be? You are the most interesting

cowboy that we have ever met. Isn't that right, Billy?"

"Uh-huh. You certainly are," Billy agreed. "Tell you what – if you want a woman who is not fussy and who thinks you're great, you could consider Mama. She likes you and she's lonely. And we wouldn't mind living here at the ranch."

"No, we wouldn't," Wyatt echoed. "Think about it."

Tom's jaw dropped. How did he get embroiled in such talk with two little boys? He was not looking to get involved with another woman ever. Especially not with Lottie Donovan. She was cute and his body seemed to agree eagerly, but after what he'd been through with Faith Parker, the embarrassment of being found lacking and then abandoned… No, thank you. No other woman would ever make a laughingstock of him. Time to change the subject.

"How about, you boys tell me where you found the piece of jewelry."

Wyatt searched his pockets and took out a dubiously clean neckerchief. From it, he revealed an ornate silver piece of jewelry with a large turquoise stone in the center. "It looks like a brooch. If no one here lost it, maybe it is old and we could give it to Mama." Wyatt looked at Tom expectantly.

Tom picked it up. It was intricately made and the remaining particles of dirt couldn't hide the exquisite workmanship. "This, my dears, is not a brooch. It's a bolo tie worn by western men, and most probably made by a Native American artist. The fact that you found it here is a mystery indeed because I don't remember any of my men wearing it. Needless to say, it is not a family heirloom either. I'll have to make some inquiries, and so I'll keep it for the moment, you understand."

Both boys nodded in agreement, although a little disappointed. Ah, the Christmas gift for their Mama. Good idea. She deserved something nice and Tom intended to buy her a present for all her efforts to make his house a home. Yes, good idea. "In exchange, I suggest the three of us go to town tomorrow and you'll pick a gift of your choice for your mother. My treat as compensation for the bolo tie that you found. What do you say?"

The idea of going shopping in town cheered them up, and jumping with the energy only seven years old have, they went to admire the newly born calf that was mooing piteously trying to get up.

A smiling Tristan went to clean himself at the utility sink in the tack room.

Tom followed him. "Thanks for saving my calf. You're the best."

"You're welcome. I hope Lottie convinced you to come to the Old Man's birthday's party next weekend."

"Yeah, she did," Tom grumbled. "I swear that woman could move mountains, she's so determined."

"Lottie has a heart of gold. I'd hate to see her hurt."

It surprised Tom that the mildly mannered veterinarian felt the need to warn him off. And for some unknown reason, it annoyed him. "As if I could hurt her. She has her way in everything and my men look at her like the sun rises with her in the morning. Of course, her fluffy vanilla flavored pancakes might be part of the reason. But the fact is that she rules my house the way she sees fit."

Tristan searched his face. "And you don't like it?"

Tom waved his hand. "How could I not? Some order and good food were needed in this house, but…"

"But you feel you're not in control any longer," Tristan said laughing. "Get used to it. We all lose control at some point in life."

"Oh, this is only temporary, until after the New Year when Lottie will find a better house for them," Tom hastened to clarify.

"It's temporary only if that is what you want, Tom. It is fine if you want to go back to how it was before because it suits you, but just remember not to hurt Lottie. Many people might take exception to that and be very upset."

"I would never hurt Lottie or the boys," Tom bristled. The fact that Tristan thought otherwise was insulting. He would do anything in his power to protect them and keep them safe.

Tristan touched his hand. "She is very vulnerable and her life was not easy. She was not always showered with love and affection in the foster care system. She tries to please and show that she is useful at any nice gesture that comes her way. That's how she grew up. She had to give something in return for people to be kind to her. Trying to prove her usefulness comes from her survival instinct. Kindness was not for free where she came from. I'm telling you this so that you can understand her better. I know more because TJ told me. There are details you'd be horrified to hear."

Tom was already horrified. "Was she abused?"

Tristan paused for a moment. Then he sighed. "There are different kinds of abuse. One is condemned by the law in no uncertain terms. The other… is more difficult to detect. It's the daily harass, the hurtful words and veiled insults, the put down. But Lottie is a survivor. She managed to stay afloat and to keep her good and generous heart intact." Having said this, Tristan grabbed his vet's bag and his coat and went to his truck. "You take care." He saluted and drove away.

VIVIAN SINCLAIR

CHAPTER 13

Tom was a man with a mission. He had to discover the owner of the bolo tie who had ventured close to Tom's barn to spy on them. Why else would the intruder walk through the brush instead of driving to their front door and state his business? Tom had to talk to Virgil. Of course he couldn't do it at the dinner table. It would alarm the others.

So he had to wait patiently until his men finished eating. He even had to skip the second helping of the delicious lemon tart made by Lottie. She looked at him with worried eyes. "I hoped you liked the dessert. Was the lemon taste too strong or too tart?"

"I loved the lemon tart. It was perfect," Tom protested, trying to convince her that her dessert was very good. And indeed it was, but he had other things on his mind that needed his attention.

When the men started to rise from the table, murmuring their 'thank-yous' to Lottie, Tom signaled to Virgil, inclining his head to follow him to his office.

Once there, he closed the door and took a seat in his chair behind the desk.

Virgil looked around at the shelves full of an assortment of books, old, leather-bound, mixed with old ledgers and spiral binders and newer paperbacks. There was still a faint smell of the cigars Tom's father used to smoke.

"Interesting smell of tobacco. Not unpleasant. I always associated it with libraries and mysterious old tomes," Virgil said.

"Yes, it permeated the books and it's still present here in this room," Tom explained. "My old man used to smoke. It didn't help him when he had pneumonia and it was his undoing in the end."

"Yeah, those were the times when most people used to smoke," Virgil said nodding in understanding.

Tom crossed his arms over his chest and looked at Virgil. "What's this I hear about you and Brianna?"

Virgil raised his head surprised. "There is no Brianna and me. Never was. Never will be. She can't stand the sight of me," he explained bitterly. "She told me I'm the ugliest man alive."

"Well, at least she didn't tell you that you're dull and boring," Tom replied. His sister worked hard, as hard as any ranch hand, and she could be blunt and cutting when annoyed. Why was she rude to Virgil, who had never hurt anyone and was always polite and ready to help? It was true that Virgil was curious about everything and stuck his nose where he shouldn't, but that was not a reason to treat him roughly. Tom could never understand women, including his own sister.

"So you see, Boss," Virgil continued in the same sad tone. "…there is no reason for you to worry. I am a poor, ugly cowboy and I'll never amount to much. I am aware of this and I know I'm not worthy of Miss Brianna, but I will watch over her even if this makes her mad at me. I will never let any handsome cowboy charm her with pretty words and take advantage of her," he said full of determination.

"Wait a minute, Virgil, you are not ugly. Don't sell yourself short," Tom argued. Although Virgil was not exactly ugly, more like homely, he was tall and well-built by years of hard physical work on the range. "You are an honest, hard-working man."

Virgil looked at him with disbelief. "Are you telling me…," he asked hesitantly. "…that you would not mind my courting your sister?"

"Yes, I don't see anything wrong with you." Tom realized that this was the truth. Virgil was a good, reliable man and Tom trusted him with his sister. Now, was Virgil able to control the spitfire that was Brianna? Probably not.

Virgil's face lit up with a huge smile. "Thank you. Of course she'll not have me, but it means a lot to me that you appreciate me."

Poor Virgil. Not many people had given him praise or even simple kind words. "I think you're a great guy Virgil. If Brianna can't see this, then it's her loss. I can't change her mind. Heck, I can't even try, she has always been very determined. Women are strange creatures and very different from us. Trust me, I discovered this the hard way and since then, I decided to steer clear of them."

Despite his curious nature, Virgil didn't ask him for more details. Or maybe he already knew the story. Tom's unfortunate love for Faith Parker was common knowledge.

"Let's talk about something else. Did you discover anything about the intruder who came so close to the outbuildings of the ranch?"

"Not much. He had the same distinct footprint that we saw close to Outlaw's Rocks. He took a large detour to avoid being seen, and reached the secondary road, which was plowed and dry, but I guess there was a truck waiting there. His footprints there blended with another man wearing city footwear. The other man was probably waiting for him and they drove off together. They were certainly not locals."

Tom searched his pockets and produced the bolo tie. "When you went to investigate, the two little boys followed you to the brushes beyond the barn. Look what they found there in the dirt." Tom pushed the bolo tie over the desk. "Have you ever seen this before? Does it belong to any of our men?"

Virgil picked up the silver object and looked at it with undisguised interest. "Beautiful. And very valuable, if I'm not mistaken. It's a unique piece. Yes, I've seen it before. This belongs to a cowboy working at the Maitland ranch. His name is John Longlegs."

"Longlegs, hmm, I've heard of him. He is Native American. Do you have any idea what he was doing behind my barn?"

Virgil shook his head. "I can't imagine. But I can tell you that he is a good, reliable cowboy. He doesn't shy away from the hardest work and I would trust him to guard my back in a critical situation. He is sort of quiet and mostly keeps to himself."

"I see. I believe you. However, he was in the brushes, watching the house, without letting us know of his presence. I understand quiet, but this is downright weird." Tom scratched his head and blinked. His eyes itched and he thought that he needed glasses. It was difficult to accept that. Glasses were for a middle aged man, not a vigorous cowboy working on the range.

"I suggest we go to Circle M ranch and ask

Longlegs what he was doing here. Or if he was even here at all," Virgil added looking at the bolo tie again.

Tom nodded. He had to get to the bottom of this story. No matter how much he disliked the idea of going on Raul Maitland's turf, he had to do it.

Early next morning, Tom and Virgil drove to Circle M ranch. The air was frigid and when Tom inhaled deeply, he felt it cut into his lungs. The secondary road was plowed, but a fresh layer of snow covered the ground. This was a harsh land. Unforgiving. And Tom loved it fiercely. This little corner of the world was his. His ancestors had struggled to coax a living out of this land, to raise fine cattle.

Next to him, in the passenger seat, Virgil was munching on an almonds and poppyseed muffin he had pilfered from the breakfast table. Lottie had baked them before dawn, because she knew Virgil was partial to them. Tom himself liked the blueberry kind.

At breakfast, Tom had gulped his coffee quickly and had not eaten anything. He was not looking forward to this visit and he was in a rush to find Longlegs before he started work or left who knew where. Tom looked at Virgil, who was humming to himself while eating his muffin. "Must you be so chirpy in the morning?" he asked.

Virgil swallowed his last bite and smacked his lips with satisfaction. "Yep, chirpy, that's me. And do you know why? Because I don't have to worry. I got nothing to lose. I got nothing, period." He laughed at his own joke. "And Miss Lottie's muffins are delicious." He leaned over to impart a secret. "I have one for you too. To sweeten your mood. If this doesn't cheer you up, then I don't know what could. Miss Lottie's food is manna from heaven."

A muffin sounded great to Tom and his empty stomach growled with approval. Keeping his eyes on the road and one hand on the wheel, he accepted the offered muffin and bit into it with relish. It was moist and flavored with almond and vanilla. It was delicious. "That's why you boys like her. Because she feeds you good food," he mumbled between two bites.

Virgil thought about this. "Of course, we are all spoiled by the food she cooks. But we like her because she is a natural nurturer. She not only cooks, but takes care of us all and frets about us. Yesterday, she ran after Angel with a woolen scarf and tied it around his neck so he wouldn't catch a cold. You know Angel. Big as a mountain and strong as an ox. This summer in Cheyenne, I saw him taking on four drunken rodeo cowboys and making mince meat out of them. He is a tough one. Yet he blushed like a schoolboy and patiently let Miss Lottie bundle him up with that scarf. Most of us are drifters. We have nothing and no one. It was a surprise to see that she cares, genuinely cares about us. We enjoy how she fusses over us, because nobody ever did. Nobody cared if we caught a cold."

Tom swallowed the last of his muffin, picked also the few crumbles left in the napkin and sighed. Yes, it was true Lottie was one of a kind person, good and caring, a nurturer as Virgil said.

Circle M ranch was in a flurry of morning activities. In front of the barn, Raul Maitland and his brother Lance, both were mounted and ready to ride.

Great – Tom thought – if I had come ten minutes later, then maybe I wouldn't have met them. But then I probably would have missed Longlegs too.

Raul spoke to Lance and dismounted, waiting for Tom to get out of his truck.

"Tom," Faith came out of the house, her dark hair unbound, her cheeks rosy from the cold, green eyes sparkling. She was a vision indeed and for the second time that day, Tom's lungs constricted and he lost his breath.

"Are you going to stand there ogling my wife or are you going to talk business?" Raul asked him.

It was Virgil who answered him. "Well Maitland, Miss Faith is a beautiful woman. You'd think by now you'd be used to men ogling her." He smiled at Faith with good-natured humor. "And who do we have here?"

Perched on Faith's hip was a toddler making impatient noises and raising his arms to Raul to be picked up. The kid had Raul's darker complexion and Faith's green eyes.

Faith laughed. "This young rascal is Elliott Ray Maitland. We intended to name him Ray, but everyone started calling him Little Elliott. So, I guess, that is his name."

Raul's face softened when he raised his son high in the air playing with him.

"He wants to get up on your horse," Faith explained. "But not today. It's cold and windy." She turned to Tom. "Tom, I'm so glad you came to visit us. Did you bring Lottie too?"

Tom shook his head. "This is not a social visit, Faith. I came with business."

She seemed disappointed. "Oh, I see. But you'll come Saturday to the Old Man's birthday party. Carmelita is cooking up a storm. It's a big event. He is seventy. I remember the Gormans never missed a party in our neighborhood."

In fact, the opportunities to socialize were so few and far between in this sparsely populated part of Wyoming, that people were eager to socialize with their neighbors especially in winter when the weather didn't always allow work outdoors. Cabin fever pushed people to meet and have fun.

Raul returned the protesting toddler to Faith and after she said Good-bye and went back into the house, he scrutinized Tom with narrowed eyes. "Well now, we are alone. What is this business you need to talk to me about?" They both knew that regardless of the personal animosity between them, in case of danger they would help each other unconditionally. It was the unwritten law of the west. Neighbor helped neighbor in order to survive.

CHAPTER 14

"We want to talk to one of your men, John Longlegs," Tom answered Raul, looking beyond his shoulder at the two cowboys that exited the barn. He knew Lucky, Maitland's foreman, but not the other, a tall, thin cowboy, strutting around, just a tad overdressed for a day of work, and in general looking like a man with an attitude.

"Why? Why do you need to talk to him?" Raul asked, unaware that Tom's attention was elsewhere.

The cowboy pushed up his Stetson and sneered. Tom felt Virgil stiffen.

"Did you hire him recently?" Virgil asked Raul, pointing with his head toward the cowboy. As if knowing they were talking about him, the cowboy saluted in a mocking way. Then he said to Lucky "I'll be back by noon," and he climbed into a rusty truck and drove off.

"I repeat, why did you come here asking questions about my men? Before answering, I want to know why," Raul said, looking at his horse, tied to a post in front of the barn waiting for him. He was starting to lose his patience. "Look Virgil, I've known you from awhile back when you worked for Parker. I don't know what your beef was with Lucky, or maybe with me, that you left to work for Gorman, but if you come here asking questions, then you have to explain yourself first."

Virgil raised his hand in agreement. "You're right, Maitland. The cowboy who just left was pestering Miss Brianna after the Christmas pageant at the school auditorium. I didn't like the pushy, disrespectful way he treated her. That's no way to court a woman in these parts of the country, if courting was what he was doing. And I told him so. I was just wondering about him, that's all."

Tom stifled a sigh. Virgil wore his heart on his sleeve. If he was not careful, people might start poking fun at him and at his unrequited love for Brianna.

Raul raised his eyebrow and measured Virgil. To give him his due, he didn't make any comment. "Joe Brown is his name, real or not. He came here this summer and I hired him at Lucky's recommendation.

Lucky knew him from his rodeo days."

"Ah, a rodeo cowboy." Virgil said, like this explained everything. There was nothing wrong with being a rodeo cowboy, but they tended to be show-offs.

Raul nodded. "In fact, when he started working for me, he said it would be only temporarily and then he would leave for another competition. That was last summer and he's still here. He stayed even over the holidays, when there is not much work and some of the men go home. I guess he had nowhere to go or Mama's cooking kept him here longer." He shrugged. "He's not the best, but he does what he is told and stays out of trouble. That's more than I can say about other men. As long as he does that, he is welcome here."

"Yes, well, see that he keeps his distance from Miss Brianna," Virgil grumbled.

It was time for Tom to put an end to Virgil's inquiry. "The truth is we came to talk to Longlegs about an entirely different matter," he said. "As my neighbor, you should know that a week ago, we found footprints in the snow close to the Outlaw's Rocks and an abandoned camp. None of my men wear boots like the ones that made these prints. It's never good news when a stranger starts roaming the more remote corners of our land."

"If you think Longlegs is roaming your land for nefarious purposes, then you're dead wrong. I would trust him with my life and that of my family. He's proven himself trustworthy many times," Raul protested.

Tom searched his pockets for the bolo tie. "Yesterday, Lottie's two boys followed Virgil in the brush beyond my barn and they found this in the dirt." He showed Raul the bolo tie.

"And prints," Virgil filled in. "The same footprints were in the slush after the snow partly melted." Virgil was one of the best trackers in this area. He could track a person like a bloodhound.

Tom continued. "Virgil remembers that he saw Longlegs wearing this intricate silver piece. We want to talk to him."

"Yes, the bolo tie is his," Raul admitted. "I don't know why you found it near your barn. By all means, let's ask him what he knows. He's in the tack room."

Coming closer to the barn, Raul patted his horse's neck, untied him, and led him inside. It was bound to be a long talk. No sense in letting the horse freeze outside.

When they entered the tack room, Longlegs was mending an old saddle. He stopped working and nodded at Virgil in acknowledgement, but otherwise he was inscrutable.

"These people have something to ask you," Raul said, coming to stand near his man in a show of support.

Tom extracted the bolo tie from his pocket. "Does this belong to you?"

A slight flicker of emotion crossed the man's face. Then it was gone. "It was made by my grandfather. He was a silversmith back in New Mexico. It's all I have left from him. For me, it's priceless."

He made no move to take it, until Tom pushed it over the table toward him. "Then it's a good thing that we found it. A man needs his keepsakes to remind him of his family and what is important to him." Longlegs took the silver piece and touched reverently the intricate design and rubbed the large turquoise stone in the center.

Tom continued, "Perhaps you can enlighten us about how you lost this valuable object in the mud beyond my barn."

"Is that where you found it?" he asked. At Tom's nod, he explained. "I lost it at the Christmas concert. When it ended and people rushed out of the auditorium, I felt a bit overwhelmed. I dislike crowds and tight spaces. I felt that I was suffocating and I took it off to open my shirt at the neck. By the time I was outside, breathing the fresh air, I realized I didn't have my bolo tie. I waited until the auditorium was empty and then I retraced my steps back, but I never found it. Somebody must have picked it up."

"Maybe it was the new cowboy who was bothering Miss Brianna." Virgil became excited by this idea.

"There were hundreds of people there. It could have been anyone," Tom added trying to temper him down. He was disappointed that he had reached a dead end.

"Because you returned this precious object to me,

I'm going to tell you something else." Longlegs looked Tom straight in the eye. "It might or might not be important. Waiting a long time in my car in the parking lot after the Christmas concert, I noticed many interesting things. There are two men following your woman."

"My woman?" Surprised Tom wondered what Longlegs was talking about. Faith? No, he couldn't have meant Faith. Brianna was his sister. Oh… "Lottie is not my woman," he said.

"She lives with you. She takes care of you. In my book, that means she is your woman." Longlegs reasoned.

Raul smiled under his thin moustache. "You bet everyone around says so. And you'd better take good care of her, Gorman. She is a dear friend of my wife. You wouldn't want to upset Faith. I might not like it."

"She lives with me… I mean, at my ranch, because her house sold too quickly and she needed time to find a suitable house."

"And you have a hotel for homeless, single women," Raul said enjoying teasing Tom and seeing his discomfort.

"Now see here, Maitland…" Tom bristled.

"Wait!" Virgil raised his voice and came between them. When they paused, he looked at Longlegs. "What men are following Miss Lottie?"

"I don't know their names. Besides, this is the west. We don't ask many questions and if we do, then the answer will be… Joe Brown. People are entitled to their privacy. What I can tell you is that both men had seen better days. They looked scruffy among people that made an effort to dress in their best clothes for the concert. One man was young, in his early twenties and dressed like a cowboy, with the shifting eyes of a man on the run."

"Do you think he escaped from prison?" Tom asked.

"I don't know that, but at least he, if not both of them, had been in prison."

"How do you know that?" Virgil asked.

Longlegs hesitated before answering. "Because of a tattoo he had on his hand."

"What about the second man?"

"The other man was a bit older, in his thirties and he looked very different. He had a beer belly and he had a tendency to turn his head from side to side."

"To look around, you mean."

"No, it was more like a nervous habit. Reflexive movements like that are a sign of a nervous, anxious nature. He was almost bald and dressed like a city man. I mean this is Laramie, Wyoming. Who in his right mind wears slacks instead of jeans, unless he's going to a funeral or in front of the judge?"

"True." Virgil nodded.

"So, I think they just recently ganged up together. I don't know why they watched Ms. Donovan, but I'm positive they did."

"Maybe they knew her from before," Virgil said. "But why not approach her directly? Why spy on her?"

"You have to ask Lottie if she noticed any cars following her to and from school or while in town." Raul said. "Besides, women have a way of coaxing secrets from us and then confessing to other women." The men looked at him mystified. "Faith told me, that she heard from Eleanor, Tristan's wife, who heard from her husband, and finally who got this from TJ Lomax in one of his visits to the vet clinic with his dog… you know his dog Goldie is getting old and…"

"Forget the dog. What did Faith tell you?" Tom interrupted him, impatient.

"I was getting there. Lottie showed TJ threatening messages she found left in her windshield. It's a secret, but Faith told me this because she was worried about Lottie."

"I'll talk to TJ. One way or another, I'll get to the bottom of this," Tom said.

Longlegs nodded his agreement. "A man has to protect his woman."

CHAPTER 15

Her cell phone rang just when Lottie was taking out of the oven a pan with freshly baked snickerdoodle cookies, which were Angel's favorite. He was such a gentle, shy man. The others reminded her without hesitation what their preferences were, Virgil liked the almond and poppyseed muffins and chicken dumplings, Hank ate everything with tomato sauce on it and preferred spicier foods. Brianna was game to try more unusual and ethnic foods, like Thai noodles or Moroccan couscous. Chris was rather picky and never ate much. Lottie had to guess what foods might tempt him. And Tom had a well-known sweet tooth and adored her cupcakes.

Only Angel never asked for anything. He enjoyed whatever she placed in front of him at the dinner table and polished off his plate. Lottie had to ask him several times about his favorites until he shyly confessed that snickerdoodle cookies reminded him of his childhood home and of his late mother who had some German ancestors. So now Lottie had baked a batch of cinnamon spiced cookies for him.

The phone rang again and Lottie almost dropped the hot pan in her haste to place it on the trivet on the countertop.

"Hello," she answered distractedly, trying to lift each cookie and place it on the rack with only one hand.

"Charlotte, it is about time you answer the phone."

Lottie grimaced. Talking to her sister-in-law Alicia was never fun. She always complained about something. Lottie would have been better off not answering at all and letting the call go to voicemail. Unfortunately, her deeply ingrained tendency to comply with demands was stronger than reason. "Alicia, I was busy cooking."

"I will be brief. It is almost Christmas and I think you should send the boys here to be with their family and to see the ranch that will belong to them one day."

Alicia's frosty tone was so devoid of any emotion that what she said didn't make sense to Lottie. When she finally understood, she was outraged. Alicia was still trying to take Lottie's children away.

"The boys and I are spending Christmas with friends, here at home in Wyoming," Lottie answered.

"I heard you were living with a man there."

Lottie had had enough of her accusations and veiled threats. "You heard gossip and immediately assumed it was true."

"I heard that you sold Wyatt's house and moved in with a man. And Wyatt has been in the ground for less than a year. Are you telling me it's not true?" Alicia's tone changed from frosty to prosecutorial.

Lord, give me strength, Lottie prayed. "First, I sold our house because it was too big, not that it's any of your business. Wyatt passed away almost two years ago, and nobody from your family bothered to come to his funeral. Second, I'm spending the holidays with a family friend of ours. There are two men and a woman in the house and three ranch hands here. Did your informant tell you to which man he was referring?" Lottie took a deep breath. "Again – this is nobody's business but my own. And now I think we should say Good-bye."

"Wait! Are you going to send the boys to us for Christmas?"

"No. The answer is no. Not now, not ever."

"We'll see," Alicia sniffed. "A judge might decide differently. We are the boys' closest relatives and we certainly have more to offer them."

"Don't you dare threaten to take away my children, Alicia. I can fight back. Wyatt was aware of the unavoidable dangers of his job as a police officer. He made a will in which he wrote clearly that I'm to have custody of the boys and that in case something happens to me too, then my uncle TJ Lomax is to be their guardian. Wyatt never talked about what caused the rift between him and his family, but he mentioned in his will that his children are not to be raised by his family in Texas under any circumstances." Lottie heard Alicia crying. "I'm sorry. I realized he'd been right when I let you all know that Wyatt was killed in the line of duty and nobody from your family came to his funeral."

Alicia started to talk haltingly. "Wyatt was

always rebellious and Dad was... somewhat autocratic. He liked things done his way. It didn't help that Wyatt was not interested in our ranch. An anomaly, but there you have it. You see, for Dad, the ranch was sacred. It came first and it was the only thing worth living for. Wyatt told him many times and in no uncertain terms that he couldn't care less about the ranch and that he could hardly wait for the day when he finished high school and was free to go away. Although I don't know what caused him to grab his duffel and leave, the differences were irreconcilable."

"What about your mother?"

Alicia hesitated. "Mama never contradicts Dad and humors him in all his decisions. You'd think she is a meek wife, but actually, she lives her own life the way she sees fit. She has her circle of friends at the Country Club, her bridge nights, her days of shopping in Dallas, and so on. She never interferes with Dad's way of ruling the house, the ranch or ...us. Dad is stubborn, but Wyatt's death shook him."

"I'm sorry," Lottie repeated and she really was.

These people had squandered their chance to be a happy family together. How sad. "Listen, the children are mine. I'm going to raise them with love and to take care of them the best I can. You have to understand that you can't have them. However, if you or anyone from your family wants to see them or to get to know them, then you are welcome here."

"I can't have children," Alicia whispered.

"You can adopt."

"I'm afraid Todd will divorce me."

"Why are you afraid? If he divorces you, then he's not worth it. You are better off without him. You are a strong person, Alicia. If you want to be a mother, not in order to keep Todd, but for yourself, because you want it, then there are a lot of orphan children in desperate need of a real family. Go look into the state care system and you'll see. There is a little boy or girl there that is the right one for you, a child that almost lost all hope of finding someone to love him."

"You were such a child, Lottie," Alicia said softly.

"I was an orphan at six. For a while, I'd hoped that I'd be adopted, but I lost that hope. I was a pudgy, short girl, not very pretty, and only the good-looking children had a good chance of being adopted. I moved through five foster care homes until I was eighteen and free to go on my own. I made my own way in life, and to be entirely honest, I had the help of some good people, Uncle TJ among them. He was the guardian angel of the orphan children."

"Is that when you met Wyatt?"

"I met Wyatt my junior year in college at the diner where I was cooking and waitressing. He was already a policeman. We discovered that we had several things in common. We were alone in the world, determined to make our own way, and needing a kindred spirit to share life's burdens and joys."

"Did you love him?"

"Oh, yes. I loved him so much. And the two boys completed our small family."

"Do you remember him? Do you go to the cemetery on the anniversary of his death? I'm sorry this question is rather morbid, but I want to know if Wyatt is remembered."

"Not the day of his death, no. On his birthday, the boys and I get a big bunch of flowers, cake and candles, and we go to the cemetery to remember Wyatt as he was in life, a healthy, vibrant, young man and loving father. Each of the boys has a favorite picture of him in their room, but I don't make a shrine in my house. Life goes on and my boys need to enjoy a normal childhood, playing, laughing, making friends."

Lottie looked outside and saw Tom lifting Billy in his arms and shaking him playfully, making the boy laugh in delight at this new game. Wyatt Jr. was chasing his puppy Tiger, who was running after a barn cat. A baby goat was butting Wyatt Jr., begging for attention or for a carrot.

Her children were healing after the shock and grief of losing their father. Life here at the ranch was good for them – Lottie thought, admiring Tom's tall, strong figure. He was a splendid man. He had always been incredibly handsome. In high school, Lottie had been hopelessly in love with him. Now, she was in danger of losing her heart to him again, if she was not careful. She was a mature reasonable woman, but her foolish heart was still vulnerable to Tom Gorman's charm.

Echoing Lottie's thoughts, Alicia asked, "What about this man you're living with?"

To her big surprise, Lottie found herself answering honestly. "I was in love with him in high school. He did us a big favor by inviting us to stay at his ranch when our house sold in only two days after listing it for sale. Spending the holidays here was a godsend. Other than that, he is the same good-looking man and very much in love with his beautiful ex-fiancée, who married another man. As for me, unfortunately, I'm still the same overweight frumpy woman. Time didn't transform me into a swan. No miracles here. However, I intend to spend a marvelous Christmas with this family. We all deserve this break from life's hardships. And the boys are having a blast on the ranch, riding and chasing after the animals."

Alicia sniffed and after a while said, "It was good to talk to you Lottie. Thank you."

"You're welcome." And Lottie discovered with surprise that she meant it.

"I'll call again, if I may."

"Of course. As long as you abandon your outlandish plans to take my boys away from me, I would enjoy talking to you again."

They hang up and Lottie was distracted again admiring Tom's athletic body. She meant to scold him for not telling anyone where he disappeared the entire morning. Hadn't he told her that the most dangerous thing here on the ranch was to get lost in a remote part of this huge deserted land, where the cell phone signal could be very weak or nonexistent? If you told no one where you were going, then good luck being found. Letting the others know where you were was a necessity not to be ignored. But did the headstrong man tell her where he was going this morning? No, he didn't.

She was so absorbed arguing with herself about this issue, full of righteous indignation, that she completely forgot she had wanted to ask Alicia who on earth kept tabs on Lottie's comings and goings in Laramie, Wyoming and then reported to the Donovan family in Texas.

CHAPTER 16

It was late in the afternoon and the cowboys were bound to return soon because the sun set early in December. Only Brianna remained at home and was keeping the boys busy, playing with an old train-toy on the carpet in the family room in front of the majestic Christmas tree and near the roaring fire in the stone fireplace.

A big pot with hearty Minestrone soup, full of vegetables, was simmering slowly on the stovetop, while spaghetti with meatballs was absorbing the tomato sauce and herbs in the oven. Humming a Christmas carol, Lottie went upstairs to Tom's room with a stack of shirts, which had just been washed and neatly folded. She pushed the door open with her elbow and entered. She stopped frozen in the doorway.

Tom, barefooted, dressed only in his jeans and naked from the waist up, was standing in front of the chest of drawers examining the content of the almost empty drawer. Doing laundry was not his favorite past time. Hearing the door opening, he frowned, annoyed that someone invaded his bedroom without knocking. He turned ready to ring a peal over the intruder's head. Then his attention focused on the stack of clean shirts in Lottie's arms and he cheered up immensely. Ah, to dress in a clean, soft shirt after a hot shower…

Tom smiled ready to thank Lottie for the shirt when he noticed her standing there like a doe in the headlights, startled, looking fascinated at his naked chest. Tom had never been a vain man. When he was younger and in love with Faith he didn't care for other women's admiration, and definitely not now, after Faith dumped him. So, becoming aware of Lottie's admiration and desire was a new and unexpected feeling. She was practically devouring his naked body with her eyes and her ardent look scorched his skin. In truth, he had never experienced before a woman having such honest desire for him.

His body answered immediately and his smile changed into a wolfish grin. "Lottie, come here." Because she showed no sign of moving, he took the shirts from her arms and dumped them on the nearest chair. Then he pulled her into his embrace, pushing the door shut. Lottie touched his feverish skin slowly, gently, with wonder, like discovering a long lost treasure.

Tom was on fire. Desire, like never before, seemed to engulf him. "Touch me, Lottie. I won't break," he said making his own explorations over her generous curves. Her petite frame fit him perfectly.

Molding her to him, Tom bent his head and kissed her. She had a very kissable mouth, with plump rosy lips. She opened to him and Tom was so caught up in his passion that he almost didn't hear the door closing down the hallway and the kids' shrieks of laughter in the family room. He looked at his inviting bed with regret and burying his face in her curly hair whispered, "Lottie, we can't continue like this. This repressed desire for you drives me crazy. My door will be open tonight and I'll be waiting for you. I pray that you'll come, but the choice is yours."

Lottie didn't need long to decide that this was her chance to know what it meant to be loved by Tom

Gorman, and she would be crazy not to grab it with both hands. She had wanted him for so long and had dreamed of what it would be like to know his passion. She was aware that he was not in love with her – how could he when he was still regretting the loss of Faith Parker – but if he wanted Lottie, and he did want her, that much was true, then so be it. Incredible as it was, Tom Gorman wanted her, short, full-figured Lottie. However, she was also aware of her not exactly attractive dumpling of a body. Only Wyatt had accepted her the way she was and for this she had been grateful and had been a good, devoted wife to him. But Wyatt was no more, and while she'd always remember him fondly, she was still very much a woman. She was alive and her desire was pushing her toward Tom.

Lottie hesitated, biting her lower lip. "With the lights turned off."

"Why? I want to be able to see you." To see her in all her womanly beauty was Tom's dream. In fact, he fantasized often about how soft she would be and how passionate when he brought her to ecstasy. Not to see her was absurd.

"Tom, you look as splendid as you looked in high school, if not better in a more mature way. I am not and have never been a classical beauty like Faith. I'd die of embarrassment to see you compare me with her and find me lacking."

"Lottie, you are very attractive the way you are and I want to see you. Trust me, I want to make this very good for you too. Come to me tonight."

Unfortunately, Billy had one of his nightmares that night and Lottie had to spend the night soothing his fears, reassuring him that everything was alright in his world. In the morning, she thought that it was foolish to have dreams and desires for a man instead of taking care of her little boys. She was a mother first and had to put her dreams to rest.

Next day, Tom drove the boys to town to give them a special treat. He lost a bet and now he had to pay, he said. More probably he wanted to buy them small gifts for Christmas, and he had no idea what they wanted.

Lottie had tried to warn him not to indulge them too much, but he was determined. Men's business, he announced to silence her. Lottie trusted Tom with her little boys, so there was no need for so much fretting and worrying or she'd become a mother-hen, holding them too close to her skirts.

She pushed aside the book she was reading and rose intent to pour some more of her favorite Jasmine tea in her mug. The kettle was kept warm on the stovetop.

The kitchen door opened and Chris came in, coughing. "It's cold outside," he said in a hoarse voice and instead of grabbing a cookie on his way somewhere else, he took a seat at the table. His coughing intensified and Lottie pushed some tissues toward him.

She poured more of the hot tea in a large mug and doctored it with lemon juice and her favorite honey. She placed it in front of him. He looked up at her. His eyes were red-rimmed and his nose was red too. Didn't these men know better than to stay outside in the frigid weather until they froze entirely and got sick?

"Coffee," he croaked.

"No." Lottie shook her head. "Drink this. Your sore throat will feel better." Quickly she made a ham and cheese sandwich because she was sure he had skipped lunch and he was too thin. To her surprise, he ate the food and drank the tea fast. She made him swallow two aspirins also.

Then, without looking at her, to her surprise he started to speak. "My mother was a drifter, moving from place to place and from town to town. She tried her best to put food on the table and a roof over our heads. Sometimes she succeeded, other times she didn't. Then we had to move fast, when our rent was due and there was no way she could pay. I was not able to have friends like other kids my age. I was always this weird new boy, avoided by most. My deafness was also a reason and the fact that I didn't encourage them to be friendly. I was tall, so no one dared bully me."

Lottie placed a hand on his shoulder and squeezed him gently to express her understanding. He had his mother, but had his childhood been happier than hers in foster care? Not by much.

"My mom worked any job she could find, waitressing or cleaning houses. Some evenings I suspect she even went out with a man from time to time. What could I say? We needed the money to survive. But she never brought any man home and she never used drugs. Also, she never abandoned me. I am grateful to her for this." He drank the last of his tea and gave the mug to Lottie. "Can I have a little more of this, please?"

Lottie poured more tea added the lemon juice and honey and placed it in front of him. "It's the jasmine from the tea with wildflowers blossom honey that has a different taste than your regular clover honey. The lemon juice with its tartness is the spice to an otherwise sweet, maybe too sweet drink," she explained looking at him so he could read her lips.

He nodded and sipped from the mug, holding it with both hands, absorbing the heat. Lottie noticed that he was not coughing so often and definitely his voice was not as hoarse as before.

"When I finished high school, I was hired as a mechanic in an auto repair shop where I had worked before during the summer and I earned more money. We were living in Cody then. Unfortunately, it was too late for my mother. I suspect she had TB for a long time because she was coughing, but we had no insurance and no money to pay the doctor. Now I had insurance, but it was too late for her. My entire life, I had asked her who my father was and stubbornly she refused to tell me. She only said that he had his own family and had no use for me. When she realized that her end was near, she finally relented and confessed that it had been a one night stand in Cheyenne, with a cowboy passing through town. She knew his name, but not much else." Chris looked at her and laughed bitterly. "As a child, I had always imagined such drama, that he loved us but couldn't divorce. I was hoping that I meant more to him, that my life was the result of a loving act, not a mere one night stand between two reckless strangers."

Lottie shook her head. "Your life is meaningful to these people no matter how it came to be. You are their brother. A deep family connection exists or Tom wouldn't have accepted you here. He is not a gullible young man."

Chris shrugged. "If you say so... After my mother died, I decided to search for him, the man who carelessly created me. It was not difficult to discover who he was. The name Gorman is well-known in these parts of Wyoming. Imagine my surprise to discover that my father was one of the richest men in this corner of the state. However, I had a good job in Cody and I came to meet him only out of sheer curiosity. To my disappointment, he had died a few years ago, without knowing he had another son."

"I guess Tom had the surprise of his life when you knocked on his door. You two don't look alike, unless you smile. Then you two have the same charming grin."

"It was a surprise. As you said, Tom is not gullible to accept the word of a stranger just because he said so. He literally grabbed my arm and drove with me to a lab in Laramie where he ordered a DNA test. Until the results came back, I stayed at the ranch, working like any cowboy. I discovered that it was hard work, but I loved riding and taking care of horses. I could talk to them without worrying that I don't hear what they say. In fact, my deafness didn't affect my life here as much as it did in town. So when the results were back and Tom had the proof that I was his brother, he insisted I stay here and I was glad to do it. I like the ranch-style life."

Lottie patted his hand. "Tom cares about you very much even if you two didn't grow up together."

Chris smiled embarrassed. "Sorry. I don't know what got into me to talk so much and to tell you all this."

"Don't you? Every person needs from time to time a friend to talk to and to unburden. And why me? Perhaps because you sensed that I can understand your problems better because I was raised in foster care. And I do. But please trust Tom and talk to him as openly as you did now. He will understand too, I guarantee it."

CHAPTER 17

It was Friday. Tomorrow would be the first day of the winter vacation. The last day of school ended earlier than usual and children ran out of school and into the cold December afternoon to meet their waiting parents.

Lottie smiled at the exuberance of the young. Had she ever been so mindlessly happy and excited? Probably not. But she hoped her children were. She turned to impart her thoughts to Faith, but Faith had stopped at the entrance to talk to the mother of a very talented girl. Instead of the nice smile of her friend, Lottie met the ugly sneer of a person she'd hoped never to see again. Her old nemesis, Doug Williams.

"Well, well, Charlotte, you rejected me because you think your cowboy is better. Soon you'll see how wrong you are." He tried to grab her arm, but Lottie had the reflexes of a lifetime, and she avoided him.

She was so focused on escaping her tormentor that she didn't see the tall figure who caught Doug's wrist in his hand like a vise. "If you have something to say, then you say it to me," Tom said quietly.

Like any bully, Doug preyed on victims he believed to be weaker than he was. Being threatened by a stronger adversary was an unpleasant surprise. "What? What do you want? Charlotte and I have known each other for a long time. Do you think you are the only one for whom she lifts her skirts?" he sneered again, trying to find his self-confidence.

Tom narrowed his eyes and squeezed his wrist. "You will never talk about Lottie like this again. Do you understand?"

Doug's astonishment made him forget his fear. "Are you crazy? You are rich and you could have any woman you want. Why would you want a frumpy, fat girl like her?" He was genuinely surprised by this turn of events.

Lottie was so embarrassed she wanted to melt into the pavement.

Hearing Doug insult Lottie made Tom so mad, he had to close his eyes for a second to calm down his temper. His squeezing intensified. "Yes, I'm crazy. But you are not to talk disparaging about her, not now, not ever. More than that, you are not to approach her ever again or you'll have to deal with me. Do you understand me?"

"Yes, I do." Doug would have agreed to anything to get his wrist released.

"And you'll never leave her threatening messages on her windshield."

Doug blinked. "I never left her any messages. Why should I? I can talk to her directly." He was a weasel and lying was second nature to him, but in this case, Lottie felt that he was telling the truth. Then who was threatening her? It made no sense.

Tom thought the same. He let go of Doug's wrist and pushed him away. "See that you do."

Finding himself free, Doug ran to the other side of the street. Rubbing his wrist, he turned back and shouted at Tom. "You think you're a hot shot? You're wrong. Your comeuppance will be soon. You have no idea whom you are pitted against." And then he ran down the street.

Later, they collected Lottie's boys from the elementary school and listened to them chattering about Christmas and their vacation. Finally, the boys fell asleep on the rear seat of Tom's truck.

Funny, Lottie thought, they had so many things to talk about and had to refrain because of the kids and now when they could talk, silence reigned in the cab. "How did you know about the threatening messages?" she asked.

"I talked to TJ and he was surprised that I didn't know." Lottie realized that he was upset, maybe even angry. "Why didn't you tell me, Lottie? Didn't you trust me to protect you?"

"Of course I trust you. But I've taken care of myself all my life since I was six years old. Also, you've been so kind to let us stay at your ranch until we'll find a new house and I didn't want to bother you with my own problems."

"You didn't want to bother me? Lottie, all the

people living on my ranch are my responsibility, whether they want this or not. It is my problem to ensure everyone's safety."

"Doug can be nasty and revengeful…" Lottie said touching his denim-clad thigh. His muscles were iron-hard and radiating heat despite the cold weather outside. Lottie withdrew her hand hastily.

Looking straight ahead at the newly plowed ribbon of the road, Tom was inscrutable. Only his voice hesitated a little before speaking. "I can deal with the Dougs of the world. He's just a bully who runs away in front of a stronger adversary." He coughed and continued. "Look, I'm a simple man, not very subtle. It was wrong of me to ask you to come to me, Lottie. I thought about it. You are a guest in my house and you shouldn't feel pressured to share my bed. No matter how much I want you, it was wrong of me to ask you. You were right not to come. At least I got your message when you didn't come." Lottie touched him again to gain his attention and he shuddered struck by a sudden thought. "Lottie, are you afraid of me? You shouldn't be. I didn't mean to …"

"Tom, stop. I'm not afraid of you, how could I be? You are kind and good-hearted. You are so patient with my boys who pestered you with all sorts of questions. I'm just afraid that you'll break my heart." Lottie laughed to cover her uneasiness. What had possessed her to tell him this?

Tom frowned. "What do you mean I'll break your heart?"

"Don't you know? All the girls were in love with you in high school. I was not immune to your charm either."

"Oh, in high school. Girls were attracted to what I represented, the typical short-famed quarterback, famous for a year or two. After I graduated, I sunk into oblivion. I didn't know you were one of those girls, who followed the football players as long as they were in full glory. They didn't know or appreciate the real me."

"You're wrong. The girls talked about the fact that you were not self-centered, despite being so handsome. Strangely, they liked you for not 'playing the field' and for sticking to your girlfriend Faith."

"Ah, Faith. She was the only one who knew the real me. I guess that's why she was not in love with me. She knew that my polish was only skin deep and in reality I was a dull fellow."

Lottie shook her head. "Faith said that there was never much passion between the two of you. That you never exchanged more than a few lukewarm kisses. Those were her words."

"Well, that's the way I am. I tried to give her room, not to pressure her to have sex with me," Tom bristled to have his former courtship for Faith described in such a way.

"Then you have changed a lot," Lottie replied. "Because we sure steam up the room every time we touch and lukewarm doesn't describe our kisses."

"I didn't change. I…" Tom scratched his head. Every time he got into an argument with women, they twisted his words. Although Lottie was right, when he had her in his arms, his blood boiled with passion. It never happened when he was with Faith. He felt this mindless desire for Lottie and only for her. And she responded to him in kind. He couldn't help grinning. She liked him. She really did.

"I wanted to come to you last night," Lottie confessed in a small voice. "Billy had a nightmare and I had to stay with him though... I've loved you since high school, Tom, but I'm a mother first. Lying there in the dark near Billy, I realized the foolishness of what I was about to do. What if people assume we are more than friends helping each other? It will create an embarrassing situation."

"I got news for you, Lottie. People, and I mean, my men, our neighbors, everyone around, they already think we are more than friends. It is unavoidable that they assume there is more going on between us. People will always gossip. Although I have never been the subject of their gossip."

"I'm sorry if our presence at your ranch placed you in a difficult position with your neighbors."

"Are you kidding? I was this stodgy, predictable rancher. Now I'll be considered more interesting after leading astray such a virtuous woman like yourself."

"You shouldn't joke about reputation…."

"Who's joking? I'm serious. I discovered I like my new self. A real Casanova, stealing kisses from unsuspecting women in the kitchen and staying awake at night anticipating they'll come to my bed. You didn't, but it was still great when I was waiting, hoping you would come."

"Are we there yet?" a sleepy voice from the back of the truck chimed in.

"Yes, we are. And your pal, Tiger, is coming to welcome you."

The little dog was tumbling all over himself in his haste to reach Billy.

"Someone left the dog out. He could get hurt running free around the yard," Lottie observed looking after the boys who were going inside.

"Not this one. He is a ranch dog. They like being underfoot all the time. Somehow they never get hurt."

Lottie nodded. "I hope the pot roast I left this morning in the slow cooker is ready."

Virgil heard her and answered from the porch. "Yes, Miss Lottie. At least I think so, considering that the entire house smells divinely of garlic and roasted meat."

"Lottie," Tom stopped her. "Just so you know, I'll be waiting again tonight," he whispered for her ears only. He loved to see her blush, he thought, looking after her disappearing inside. He turned to Virgil, who was grinning from ear to ear. "What? Stop showing your teeth, Virgil. Better tell me what happened in my absence."

"Angel was following a mountain lion and he was shot at. I went to investigate and found some traces as fresh as yesterday probably. They were at the camp at Outlaw's Rocks. But the camp was deserted."

"Ah, so there is another one hiding on my land." Tom explained to Virgil about his encounter with Lottie's old relative from foster care.

That night, after every one had retired to their rooms and silence reigned over the house, Lottie tiptoed to the boys' room and assured herself that they were sleeping peacefully. She pulled the cover more tightly around their little bodies and then went to the family room where she left the tree lights on every night. In the fireplace, the flames had died down, but the ashes remained red.

"Come here, love," Tom's voice startled her and made her jump.

"Tom, I had no idea you were here." Lottie pressed her hand over her heart, and came closer to the chair where he rocked slowly. He tugged at her hand to come even closer and lifted her onto his lap.

He buried his face in her hair. Her womanly scent was stirring his desire. She was so cuddly and soft and her skin felt like velvet under his touch.

"The tree is beautiful," she said nestling in his arms.

"Beautiful," he repeated inhaling deeply and trailing his mouth from the sensitive skin below her ear to her neck. "Do you want me, Lottie?" he asked softly against her neck.

She raised his face and looked at him. "I've

wanted you for a long time, Tom. Only in my dreams. I've never confessed this to anyone. I've never even admitted it to myself."

"Why not?"

"Because I don't have hopeless dreams. I have real, achievable goals."

It was shocking for Tom to realize he had been her dream. He opened his mouth to ask why she'd never told him. Because he had been in love with Faith and she'd married another man.

He might be clueless, but now he did what seemed right. No more talking. He picked her up and carried her to his room. He was done waiting and questioning what he should do.

He deposited her on his bed and when she looked up alarmed and demanded he turn off the lights, he only smiled and showed her the pleasure he had in exploring her body and kissing her milky white skin. After a while, caught up in the overwhelming wave of passion, Lottie forgot about the lights. Besides she liked to look at Tom's body too, all hard muscles from hard work.

And when the moment of ecstasy came, Tom covered her moth with his own to prevent her cries of delight from becoming too loud and he lost himself in the pleasure of her body.

CHAPTER 18

For the first time in a long while, Lottie woke up feeling pleasantly warm and safe. No more cold feet and cold sheets and loneliness that threatened to break her heart. A strong arm kept her tightly anchored to a warm body that radiated heat like a furnace. If this was a dream, then she didn't want to wake up.

She blinked, disoriented and the first thing she saw was an alarm clock on the nightstand that glowed in the dark, showing it was close to 4 am. She tried to get up, but the arm tightened around her middle.

"Tom," she whispered his name to assure herself that she didn't dream this wonderful night in her otherwise bleary existence.

He kissed her nape. "Go back to sleep, Lottie. It's still early."

"It's 4 am."

"I know. In summer, we wake up even earlier than that. Now in winter we can sleep more."

Reluctantly, she got up. "I have to go. I don't

want the boys to wake up and not find me in my bedroom.

He couldn't argue with that. After pulling her back for a last kiss, he let her go.

Lottie tiptoed down the hallway, when a voice behind stopped her frozen on the spot. "Well, well. I guess you'll tell me you are sleepwalking and by chance happened to walk into my brother's bedroom…," Brianna said peering in the semi-darkness at Lottie.

Horrified that she'll awaken the whole house, Lottie turned back to face her. "Shht! Not so loud… I… I'm…" She shook her head. Then she straightened her spine and told Brianna, "Come with me to the kitchen if you can't sleep."

"In summer, we all wake up at four. In winter, I envy the others who can sleep longer. My inner clock wakes me up at the same hour every day," Brianna explained following Lottie to the kitchen, curious to hear how she would explain her presence in Tom's room.

On her way to the kitchen, Lottie peeked into the boys' room and saw them sleeping peacefully. In the kitchen, she turned on the stove and prepared a pot of tea. She placed in front of Brianna a steaming mug and a plate with oatmeal raisin cookies. "Jasmine tea."

"I don't drink tea. Especially not in the morning," Brianna protested.

"You do now. Drink while it's hot."

Brianna raised her eyebrows. Lottie was not usually so forceful. "Okay, Miss Morality, explain. Not what you were doing with my brother. Your presence in his room is self-explanatory, but why? I know he was looking at you like you were the second best thing invented after... cupcakes, but why did you give in to him?"

"When you surprised me in the hallway, the first thing that came to mind was an excuse. I almost said 'I'm sorry', but I realized I'm not. Whatever I feel about tonight, and I still have to think it over, I know I'm not sorry. You almost make it sound promiscuous. It's not. Not for me. I've loved Tom since I was in high school."

"You're kidding. Were you one of the football groupies, who followed him at every game?"

Lottie laughed. "No, of course not. I admired him from afar. I was a frumpy teenager, dressed in hand-me-down clothes. I was not one of the cool girls. They had no chance either because Tom had eyes only for Faith Parker. They were a superb, perfect couple."

"Right. I can see how perfectly it turned out for them," Brianna scoffed.

Lottie shrugged. "Life is unpredictable. As for me, how could I regret last night? It was everything I dreamed of and more."

"I'm sorry to tell you this, but it is possible that nothing will come of it," Brianna said gently.

"I know. Tom is still upset for losing Faith."

"No, I don't think so. He's using Faith as an excuse not to get involved. He's stuck in a mire of his own making and it's impossible for him to get out of it. He is a very good rancher, very competent, and has no problems making the best decision quickly. But he is lethargic and clueless in his personal life."

"I know, Brianna. I'm aware nothing will come of it. I'll always come up short compared to Faith. But at least I'll have the memory of this incredible night."

"Pshaw! You're twice the woman Faith is. If only my idiotic brother could see it."

Lottie patted her hand. "It's nice of you to say so. We considered Faith arrogant and snotty in high school. She's not. She is a wonderful person. Not only beautiful and talented, but also strong and brave, ready to fight an army for what she considers right."

"Why do you think she married Raul Maitland?" Brianna asked genuinely puzzled. "He is wealthy, but not wealthier than Tom, not by much. He will be after he adds the Parker land to his holdings. But Tom is much more handsome."

"Yes, Tom is more handsome, although I'm prejudiced. As for Faith, she loves Raul. Truly loves him, and she would lay her life down for him and little Elliott. But enough about Faith. How about you, Brianna? It is the hour for confessions and turnabout is only fair. Could you find it in your heart to look at Virgil with more acceptance, to be more open-minded? He loves you so much."

Brianna waved her hand with impatience. "Virgil is a clown. He is so curious. He sticks his nose everywhere like an old woman."

"He is an honest, hard-working man. And he had a hard life."

"Why do you have so much understanding for him?"

"Because in different ways, both of us have been orphans and had no one to call family. It's not easy to be alone in the world. Granted, Virgil can't be called handsome..."

"No, he certainly is not handsome, but that is not what I dislike about him." Brianna paused to gather her thoughts and replenished her tea mug. "You see, I love this ranch. I was born here and it's in my blood. But I'm almost thirty years old and lately I've started to feel restless. Don't misunderstand me, I'm not looking for adventure, but I feel there must be more to life than working here. Virgil is part of the same old picture, with nothing new to offer."

"Except his heart. You are right. If his heart is not

enough and not what would make you happy, then you are right to discourage him. He deserves a woman's love and a family."

"He's too poor to take care of a family. This is the reality. This is the life of a cowboy."

"How sad," Lottie said, dusting the cookie crumbles from the table.

"I'm not sure what I want. Definitely some spice, some change in the monotonous routine of daily life."

"I understand."

"It's like I was living like an automaton all these years and now I can finally see clearly and I want more. There must be more to life than this."

Lottie sighed. "Sometimes there is grief and hurt and loneliness. Then one remembers fondly the moments when life was routine, but safe."

"I'm sorry your husband was killed Lottie, but I need more."

"Of course, Brianna. You have to find your own way in life and you have to discover what makes you happy."

FOOTPRINTS IN THE SNOW

CHAPTER 19

The Maitland ranch house was decorated from top to bottom with light strings, green garlands, bells, red bows and glass ornaments. This year in particular the festive tone was raised a notch as they celebrated not only Christmas, but also the seventieth birthday of the patriarch of the Maitland family.

For a long time, the Old Man had been the most prominent rancher in the area. He was retired now, and his birthday was celebrated by the family with a large party. An open invitation had been issued to all at large, landowners and low ranch hands as well.

By mid-day, the place was packed with people, coming and going, joking, laughing, and having a good time. Of course, there were some who said that Carmelita's good food brought people here as much as the respect for the Old Man.

Elliott Maitland was sitting in the family room, in his favorite armchair near the fireplace, with his good friend and neighbor, John Parker, sitting opposite him.

His three sons, Lance, Raul, and Tristan were mingling with the guests. He looked fondly at his three daughters-in-law, beautiful Faith with the voice of an angel, classy Eleanor, who had recently been elected Judge, replacing old Judge Conrad Parker who retired, and Annie, who was playing on the floor with the children, in front of the Christmas tree. The Old Man had been blessed with grandchildren, Lance and Annie's twins, Eric and Isabella so different in personality, were playing with Raul and Faith's boy, Little Elliott. Tristan's son, Zach, was too old at almost thirteen to play with his little cousins. And tiny Miranda, blond like her mother and pretty as a doll, was watching the noisy party from the safety of her father's arms.

"Well Old Man, another year has gone by." John Parker raised his glass, recently refilled with Carmelita's special hot cider. "Happy Birthday."

"Who are you calling 'Old Man'?" Maitland grumbled watching Little Elliott pulling Poppy the bulldog to play with him. Good luck with that! The darn dog was stuffed with food from the kitchen and nothing could move him from his place on the rug, in front of the fire, where he was snoring, dreaming of his next meal.

"I don't mind that the years are passing, now that I know there is Raul to take good care of the Parker land and the future is assured by Little Elliott," Parker said looking at his energetic grandson. "Did you see him the other day on Raul's big stallion, in the saddle in front of his father, cheering the horse on? Our boy will be a great rancher, born in the saddle – as they say," he said bursting with pride.

The Old Man nodded. Little Elliott was proving to be a natural rider. "Now you see I was right when I said that Faith and Raul are made for each other. Do you still regret Faith didn't marry Tom Gorman?"

"You were right. I don't regret it. Tom is a good, hard-working rancher, but my fiery Faith would have walked all over him. Raul is…" Parker saw the heated look exchanged by his daughter and Raul. It was so intense that he blushed. Ah, he bet another grandchild would soon be on the way. A Little John perhaps.

"People say that Tom Gorman is still carrying a

torch for Faith," the Old Man said. "He had plenty of time to court her. Almost ten years and he did nothing."

"You forget his dad died and he had to learn to manage the ranch. He worked hard and did well. I can understand why courting was not first on his mind," Parker observed. "Besides, now he's got Lottie Donovan and her boys staying at his ranch. And as you said, people talk."

"Lottie Donovan, you say? Hmm! The widow of that policeman… That was a tragedy."

But Parker was distracted by Little Elliott who, tired of being ignored by the bulldog, was pulling his ears trying to make him move. Irritated, the dog was growling and Parker was afraid for the precious little boy, who was daring and jumping with both feet into all sorts of trouble.

The house was full of people, and Tom was not comfortable in a crowd. The good news was that most of them were full of food and had imbibed plenty the famous hot cider, which was doctored with alcohol. After exchanging greetings with all his neighbors and hearing opinions about the price of beef and feed for cattle, he felt slightly hot and claustrophobic, in need of a breath of fresh air. So he took his coat and made his way outside.

He saw Tristan Maitland in the barn and went there to say hello to the veterinarian. In the barn, Tristan disappeared inside one of the stalls with his children to show them the baby goats. Instead, Tom was stopped by Faith who was coming out.

"Tom, I'm glad you could come. I need to talk to you. It's about Lottie."

"What about Lottie?" Tom asked cautiously.

"Lottie is my best friend." Faith placed her hand on Tom's arm and looked at him with her cat-like green eyes. "She was the only one who welcomed me back with open arms and treated me with honesty. She is a very good person. I know she tries to be strong for her children's sake, but personally I think she is fragile and vulnerable because of growing up in the foster care system. It's amazing how such a good and worthy person can lack self-confidence."

"What do you mean? Lottie does not lack…," Tom bristled.

"Let me explain. Lottie thinks she needs to be useful and helpful in order to be accepted or loved. She was never adopted, not even considered for adoption. She had a very good marriage with Wyatt and he loved her, but she went out of her way to please him and to indulge his every whim. Like that huge house he bought, although it was beyond their financial means."

"I know. She told me," Tom answered, slightly impatient. He was uneasy to discuss Lottie's situation with Faith or anyone else. He was a private man, who didn't like airing his business or inner thoughts in public or on Facebook. Talking about Lottie with Faith was weird, even disloyal.

"In the beginning, I thought she was crazy in love with him," Faith continued. "Later, I realized that while she loved him honestly and was devoted to him and to their family, she was always waiting for the other shoe to drop. She was afraid that she would lose Wyatt. Ironically, he was faithful to her, but she lost him just the same. So, she needs a man to prove to her that he loves her unconditionally."

"And you don't think I am that man?" He asked increasingly irritated and annoyed.

"Oh, I think you are, it's just that you have a way of procrastinating, and Lottie needs a man who…."

"I think you should stop interfering, Faith. What's between Lottie and me, it's our business."

"Watch how you talk to my wife, pal. I might take exception and teach you a lesson or too," Raul said in a menacing voice, coming out of a stall.

"I'm not afraid of you, Maitland. I can fight you anytime you want," Tom answered, looking him straight in the eye. A confrontation was brewing between him and Raul, not only because Raul had taken Faith from him, but also because Tom needed to assert his strength. No one should think Tom Gorman was a weakling.

"Will you two stop this macho contest? This is about Lottie. Tom, I want to tell you to treat her with care," Faith intervened.

"Will you stop pushing this Lottie subject at me?

I make my own decisions and...," '...and my own courting' - he wanted to say, but a small cry of distress interrupted him.

At the barn door, Lottie was looking at him, her eyes wide with hurt and tears pooling at the corners. "Ah," she cried again and turning on her heels, ran away.

"Now, you see what you did?" Faith told him aghast.

Whatever he did or said, it was a misunderstanding and Lottie was not unreasonable. He had to find her and explain what he meant.

Unfortunately, the explanation had to wait. When he ran after her, he met his foreman, Hank, who was looking for him. "Boss, I'm glad I found you. Come quickly. There is a fight in the bunkhouse between Virgil and Maitland's newly hired man."

Telling himself that he'd talk to Lottie later and she would understand, Tom followed Hank to the bunkhouse. Instead of going in, Hank turned left and pushed his way through a circle of ranch hands, who were cheering loudly for the two men rolling on the frozen ground.

Joe Brown, or whatever his real name was, was thinner, but faster and fighting dirty. Virgil was stronger and whatever enraged him, made him really mad. Brown hooked his leg and pulled him down and produced a nasty looking knife. A roar went through the ranch hands. They liked a good fight, but not a dirty one. Dishonesty was not appreciated and unfair advantage was frowned upon. They seemed not to realize that this was not a simple fight for sport between two inebriated cowboys.

Tom knew. He'd seen it in Virgil's determination and he knew it was about his sister. Darn Brianna for provoking such a confrontation at this party. Because, right now, if Tom tried to stop the fight, which he could do easily, Virgil would lose the others' respect. He was not a child to be saved from a fight by the teacher.

Just then, Brown lunged and Virgil turned sideways, but not enough to avoid being cut in the arm. Tom saw that it was a tactical move as Virgil grabbed the other's hand and exerted enough pressure that Brown dropped the knife. Virgil applied a one-two to the other's jaw and stomach and left him lying there on the ground dazed. He grabbed the knife and threw it as far as he could, away from the circle of onlookers.

Brown was finished. Not only did he fight dirty, but he lost. According to the unwritten rules, he cheated them all out of a fair fight.

"Joe, you can come later to pick up your wages," Raul announced in a calm tone like talking about the weather. Then he shook Virgil's hand. "Good fight."

By the time they all went back into the house and Virgil had been patched up by Carmelita, Lottie was long gone. No one knew where she went or with whom she drove away. She and her boys had vanished.

Driving morosely to his ranch, Tom listened to Virgil's litany.

"I had to do it, Boss. I caught the weasel kissing Miss Brianna behind the bunkhouse. He laughed and said that she's primed for loving as none of the ugly cowboys on our ranch can do it properly," Virgil explained from under the raw beefsteak that covered his swollen eye.

Tom could have pointed out that Brianna had dealt before with slimy cowboys like Brown, but if Virgil felt like the self-appointed rescuer of a damsel in distress, who was Tom to argue.

Once at home, Tom ran to the kitchen, then to Lottie's room. Nothing. All their things were missing; even Tiger, the puppy, was gone.

CHAPTER 20

Tom started by calling Faith and telling her that if she had suggested to Lottie to hide at the Maitland ranch to teach him a lesson, then she was pushing him too far. Faith assured him that Lottie was not there and in fact – she confessed sheepishly – she had decided to listen to Raul and stop interfering.

"I hope I live to see the day when you stop interfering," Tom muttered and he hung up after concluding that Faith indeed knew nothing. How had Raul Maitland succeeded to bring Faith to heel, was a miracle. She certainly never listened when Tom asked her to do this or that.

Other phone calls ended similarly. No one had seen Lottie leaving and no one knew where she could be.

Tom decided to visit TJ Lomax, remembering that Lottie had intended to stay with the old curmudgeon before Tom offered his house.

"So the pigeon flew the coop. What did you do to her?" TJ asked rubbing his hands and grinning amused by Tom's predicament.

"You should know, you hid her," Tom replied angrily.

"No, I don't, and no, I didn't."

Tom had stormed into TJ's office intending to search the house from top to bottom, from the downstairs office to the small apartment upstairs. He was convinced Lottie was there and he was not going to leave before talking to her.

Now, he was not so sure and was inclined to believe TJ. The small office was crowded to the ceiling with books, files, and other stuff, lots of stuff that not even the busiest private investigator in New York City could use in a lifetime. The moment he entered the room, Tom knew Lottie was not there. Her touch was missing. There was no vanilla aroma coming from upstairs. Instead, the same slightly musty smell permeated the office.

No lights in the windows, no decorations. Only a scrawny tree tilting to one side adorned a corner of the room, and half of its lights were burnt and not working.

No angel on top.

Lottie had definitely not been here recently.

"Where do you think she is?" he asked TJ in desperation.

"I didn't know she was missing." TJ answered, continuing to grin like a fool. "Maybe she found a different house for herself and the kids," he advanced the idea.

"Nope. I checked with her realtor. It's a dead season until after the New Year. She didn't hear from Lottie. The inventory for both sale and rent is rather small. And if you don't stop grinning, I swear TJ I... I'll make you... somehow."

"He-he-he, I'm shaking in my boots. And by the way I was invited to your ranch for Christmas. You can expect me then."

"To my house? I thought you're spending all your holidays with Terror Proffitt."

"Nope. Not this Christmas. She plans to visit her sister in Florida. Lottie assured me that you will be happy to have me for Christmas."

"You're free to come,…" Now, Tom was the one grinning. "…if you are fond of Brianna's burned cooking."

TJ's face fell. "Oh, I didn't think of that."

"You'd better think and fast. No Lottie, no good food for Christmas, and no everything else that Christmas implies, gifts, carols, jokes."

"I wonder how you guys survived before Lottie," TJ observed.

That's exactly what Tom asked himself while driving back to the ranch. How did he ever survive without Lottie, without her warm smile and without caressing her silky skin at night. Dream on, boy! No silky skin and no warm smile. All because of a misunderstanding. It was true he was not a smooth talker and never had been. That's what made Faith think him dull and boring. Women liked pretty words and flowers. That's what he had to do. Maybe even learn a love poem.

The idea made him shudder, but a man's got to do what a man's got to do. Love poem it was. That British fellow, Shakespeare, had written a whole bunch of them. Love Sonnets. Tom had an old leather-bound book with them. He had to learn a poem, or at least a few verses, he amended.

And flowers, he needed flowers. These would be difficult to find now in December, but maybe he could find a potted plant at the Buds and Blossoms flower shop in Laramie. They had to sell something during the winter months too.

Some women liked jewelry and he could afford to buy, but he doubted Lottie was the kind who was crazy for jewelry. He hadn't seen her wearing any, except for her old thin wedding band. This irritated him for some reason. Her dead husband had been a hero, but two years had passed, and Lottie should go on with her life. Maybe Tom should buy her a nice ring to replace her old wedding ring, which needed to go.

Tom felt better now that he had a plan.

Once arrived home, however, the house smelled like TJ's office. No vanilla smell and no roast cooking in the kitchen either. He found his family there. Chris was rolling the dice on the table, while Angel was placing carefully on the table what was left of the cookies baked by Lottie.

At first he thought they were gambling with the cookies at stake. Not a bad idea. But no.

"I'm rolling the dice to see who is in charge of cooking starting tonight," Chris informed him.

"And I'm making an inventory of the cookies left and making rations to have until Christmas," Angel enlightened him.

Tom scratched his head. They all looked at him accusingly. No more humming carols or cheerful whistling. "Why is the radio turned off? We've always had Christmas music in the kitchen."

Nobody pointed out that they had music in the kitchen only since Lottie had come to live with them. Of course, no one objected when he turned on the radio perhaps a tad louder than usual. He looked mad enough to spit nails and they knew now was not the moment to mess with him.

"Where is Virgil?" he barked.

"He heard noise outside and went to investigate. You know how curious he is," Hank explained.

"When was that?"

The men looked at one another.

"About an hour or so ago, Boss."

"An hour to investigate a noise?"

"You know Virgil, he gets distracted by one thing or another. It's not like he had work to do at this hour."

Tom grabbed his coat again. "Angel, come with me," he said on his way out.

It was quiet in the barn and Virgil was not there. The bunkhouse was also empty.

"Where did he vanish?" Tom wondered frustrated. It was almost dark and he was not in the mood to form a search party because Virgil was curious and got lost somewhere. Not in the dead of winter. After walking for a while, Angel found some traces.

"Here, Boss. There are some footprints and not all are Virgil's." While not as good a tracker as Virgil, Angel, the mountain man, was adequate at finding a lost person.

"Let's see." The footprints were going down into a ravine that was not very steep. "Shall we take the horses?" Tom asked.

Angel was looking down and started running downhill. "Here he is."

Tom didn't see much beyond the wild brush that grew down there and which had been a nuisance several times when one of his cattle wandered down and got tangled in the brush. Darn Virgil for getting into all the places that were difficult to reach.

But he followed Angel downhill.

They found Virgil at the bottom of the ravine, trying to move an unconscious man. "Who do you have there, Virgil?"

Virgil let go of a man who fell to the frozen ground, moaning. "I found this skunk spying around the barn. When I asked him what he wanted, he said he was an old friend of Miss Lottie and he wanted to talk to her. When I told him she was not here, he gave me a message, a paper already written for her. Now I ask you, if he came to talk to her, why the written message?"

Angel produced a flashlight from his pocket and directed the light on the stranger's face, which intensified the moaning. Tom looked at him and made a disgusted sound. "This is no friend of Lottie. She knew him from her foster care days. Not pleasant memories. He was pestering her then and he continued to do it now, despite my warning to stop."

"You've met him before, Boss?"

"Oh yeah, the other day at school. It looks like my warning was not enough. Angel, call the sheriff."

"I ain't done nothing," the man on the ground cried.

"Trespassing on private property with intention of harming. Do you know that we shoot people for this?"

"You have no right…"

"I have the right to protect my land and my family. That's how we survived here for more than a hundred years."

"I have rights too. This man assaulted me," he said pointing a finger accusingly at Virgil.

"You should consider being hit by Virgil to be

child's play compared with what I'll do to you."

"Not fair. I was only giving Charlotte a message," he complained again.

"Where is the message?" Tom asked.

Virgil searched his pockets and produced a wrinkled piece of paper. "Here, Boss. I had no time to read it because I had to follow him. He had a truck waiting, but the driver took off quickly and didn't wait for him."

Tom redirected the light and perused the message. "If you care about your kids' safety, then come tomorrow to Outlaw's Rocks. Bring the ring and the bolo tie. Talk to no one or the boys will suffer." He pocketed the paper. "Angel, tie him up."

"This must be the guy hanging about Outlaw's Rocks. What ring is he talking about?" Virgil asked invigorated by the idea of a new adventure. "He doesn't know Miss Lottie and the boys are gone."

"Where did she go?" the man asked, his hands tied and the rope pulled by Angel.

"None of your business. Angel, tie him to the post

in the barn until the Sheriff arrives."

"You have no complaints against me," the man protested.

"Sure I have. Trespassing and assaulting my man here," Tom said pointing at Virgil.

CHAPTER 21

Next morning when Tom entered the kitchen, an unpleasant odor permeated the air. "What is this awful smell?" he asked instead of saying Good morning.

"Miss Brianna made pancakes this morning," Hank answered.

He looked at his men doggedly chewing what they could cut from the charred remains on their plates. "Disgusting," he said pushing his plate away.

"Watch your language, brother," Brianna admonished him, daintily nibbling on a raw carrot. "I lost at dice so it was my turn to prepare breakfast. It's either this or go hungry the rest of the day."

Tom refrained from mentioning that she was not eating the burnt pancakes. But the situation was intolerable. They were working men and needed good food and plenty of it. He needed to find Lottie and bring her back or he'd have a mutiny on his hands.

"Someone's here to see you, Boss," Virgil announced coming in.

"Now? We have to go to Outlaw's Rocks. The sheriff promised to come by."

Virgil shrugged. "He's in the family room."

Hungry and in a bad mood, Tom went to see who it was, determined to send him on his way as fast as possible.

The stranger was dressed in western garb, with expensive hand-tooled leather boots, holding his Stetson in his hand. His coat was too thin for a Wyoming winter. He was middle-aged, but holding straight. He scrutinized Tom from under bushy brows. "I'm Donovan," he announced, without moving to shake hands or smile.

"And I'm Gorman, but I assume you know considering that you are in my house," Tom answered feeling his bad mood increasing. Was this the guy who wanted Lottie's children? Could he resort to blackmail? He didn't look like someone who had spent nights in the abandoned camp at Outlaw's Rocks.

"I found out you have something that belongs to me." The older rancher told him in a superior tone.

"Look, you came into my house uninvited and

you start throwing accusations without explaining yourself. I am warning you I'm very close to losing patience and throwing you out. Talk or leave. Your choice, but do it fast."

Donovan looked at him briefly and deciding Tom was not intimidated by his brusque manner, started to explain. "I came for the boys. My grandsons are all I have left and I heard their mother sold the house from under them and they are homeless now."

"Wait a minute." Tom raised his hand, outraged on Lottie's behalf. "Their mother is a high school math teacher and very capable of buying or renting them a proper house. She is visiting here for Christmas."

"Is she your mistress?" the other man asked bluntly.

"It's none of your business…. She is my fiancée," Tom blurted out the answer, weighing the words in his mind and feeling their rightness.

Donovan raised an eyebrow. "You already gave her a ring? Isn't it too soon after my son died?"

"How would you know? Neither you, nor anyone

from your family was here for his funeral to support Lottie. She struggled all alone with her grief and with their sons' nightmares. Did you know that Billy wakes up almost every night crying and having nightmares? Have you been here to see Wyatt Jr. holding onto Lottie's hand, afraid that if he lets go, she'll disappear from their lives like his father?"

The older man looked down, twisting his hat in his hands. "I was there.... At the funeral."

"What? That is news to us all. Nobody saw you there."

"I was there. I never made my presence known. There were so many people you'd think the whole town had come. The entire Police Department was there."

"Your son was killed in the line of duty. He was a hero in this town and honored as such. Lottie was heartbroken, but she had to be strong for the boys."

"Fine words. But a dead hero is... just dead. He would still be alive today if he had worked on the ranch like all the men in our family." Resentment was mixed with grief in his words. "I lost my only son because he was a fool and chose a path that led him to destruction."

"Every man in this world is free to choose his own path."

"He made a mistake to leave Texas and our ranch."

"Whatever mistakes he made, were his to make. Besides, life is unpredictable. My old man smoked himself to an early death. It was his choice to make. No one could stop him. Your son was happy here. He liked being a policeman and he adored his family. Short as his life was, maybe he had more happiness in it than others have in a longer life."

The older man swallowed to temper down his emotion. "The boys... My grandchildren are all I have left."

Perhaps now was not the right time to tell him that the brave policeman had stated specifically in his will that the children are not to be raised by his family in Texas. The old rancher had been inflexible as a father, but now he was obviously grieving. "Listen, I can assure you, and every soul in this town can, that Lottie is a wonderful mother and the children love her. More than that, to take the boys away from her now, when they are still trying to cope with the loss of their father, would be to destroy them."

"I see. What about you? How do you figure in their life? Is she marrying you so soon because she can't manage financially?"

It was on Tom's tongue to say again, it was nobody's business. But regardless of the past, the old man was genuinely mourning the death of his son and he deserved some reassurances, if not explanations. "Her adoptive uncle is a friend of mine. As a favor to him, I invited her to live at the ranch when her house sold in two days and they had to move."

"Out of the goodness of your heart or were you lovers before?"

"Watch what you're saying. I won't take insults to her. The answer is – neither. I thought we could help each other. The boys wanted to learn to ride and I tasted Lottie's cupcakes and I was lost. She is an excellent cook and homemaker."

Donovan wrinkled his nose. "Judging by the burnt smell here, one would doubt that."

"That's my sister Brianna cooking pancakes this morning."

"Did Charlotte sleep late?"

Tom sighed. He had to tell the other man the truth. "Lottie is not here."

"What do you mean, 'she's not here'?"

Tom scratched his head. "We were at a party two days ago and we had a misunderstanding. Lottie took the boys and vanished. But I'm looking for her and when I have a chance to explain, she'll understand." Or so he hoped. Because he was lost without her. "She's not unreasonable, only sensitive about some issues. Frankly, I don't understand them well, but I'm hoping that with some love poems and flowers and a ring, she'll be more amenable."

Beginning to have a clear picture of what had happened, Donovan smiled with understanding. "Well son, you're in a pickle. When women feel they are treated unfairly, you have a long way to get back into their good graces again." He really liked this honest rancher, perhaps too honest for his own good. He still had to meet his daughter-in-law, the mother of his grandsons. "Do you have any idea where she is?"

Tom shook his head in frustration. "She was not where I thought she might be."

"What about my grandsons? Tell me about them."

"You'd be happy to know that both of them are born cowboys. They love to ride and took to the saddle with ease. In fact, the first time I met them, they offered to pay me three dollars, which was all the money they had, to teach them to ride. Wyatt Jr. is curious and eager to learn everything there is about a ranch. He tags after Virgil all day, peppering him with questions. Billy is more interested in animals. He has a puppy, Tiger, and likes to be in my sister's company who loves horses. They are both great kids."

Virgil came in, leaning from one foot to the other impatient. "Boss, the horses are ready. We need to go."

"Yes, Virgil. I'm coming." Tom turned to the

Texas rancher. "Listen, I have to go. I had an intruder last night and his partner is holed up in a remote corner of my ranch. I'm going to catch him. The sheriff promised to come too. You can sit and relax here until I'll be back. Then we'll talk some more if you want."

"An intruder? Hmm! Would you mind if I tag along with you? I'm pretty good with a rifle, but I'll need a horse."

"Aren't you tired?" Tom asked.

"Heck no. I'm a rancher. Riding all day suits me."

"Then come."

They were ready to go when Virgil said, "You know Boss, it occurred to me that the first time we were there we saw only footprints in the snow. How come he had no horse? It is too far from everywhere to simply walk there."

"Good question."

Angel, who was handing Tom a blanket and some food, looked at Virgil. "There is an old abandoned road that ends on the other side of the canyon. In winter, it's not plowed and it's impracticable. There is also a hunter's shack somewhere along this road."

"I know where it is," Virgil said. "If you go there, you have this eerie feeling that you are at the ends of the world. It is so deserted and there is no sign of a human presence as far as you can see. Some say these places are spooked or cursed."

"Superstitions, that's all," Tom concluded. "We go riding. It will take longer, but it's safer. The truck might get mired in uneven places and might be seen and heard from a distance. We would lose the advantage of surprise."

CHAPTER 22

Riding to Outlaw's Rocks, Tom told Donovan about the message meant for Lottie. The rancher was outraged. "He threatened to harm the children?"

"Yes. And he asked Lottie to bring 'the ring and the bolo tie'. I know how he got the bolo tie. It was not his and I returned it to the rightful owner. But the ring... What ring? I've never seen Lottie wearing any other ring except her plain gold wedding band."

"She's still wearing her wedding band?" the rancher asked surprised.

"Every day, although it's been two years since her husband died."

"I'm glad that she respects Wyatt's memory. And you don't have to be upset, son."

Virgil interrupted them and raised his arm. "There, to the left, those are Outlaw's Rocks. Shall we disperse and come from various directions at him?"

In the end, they decided to ride forward to see if there was someone at the rocks or not.

"Impressive geological formation," Donovan observed.

"You should see the canyon beyond it. It's very deep with abrupt, almost vertical walls."

Tom had just finished saying this, when a volley of rifle shots were fired in their direction. Virgil fell down from his horse with a loud cry.

Tom dismounted afraid for his man. "Virgil, are you badly hurt?"

Virgil opened one eye and winked at him. "Nah, it was not a good shot. I'm going to crawl and circle the rocks and get him from behind. You continue to talk to him."

Donovan took the initiative. "Hey you there! Who are you and what do you want on this ranch?"

No one came out from behind the rocks, but he answered. "Gorman, I have no beef with you. I want the woman. I have you in the range of my rifle. You don't want to die. Give me the woman."

"You didn't answer my question. Who are you and why do you want the woman?" Tom raised his voice.

"The name is O'Rourke."

Tom frowned. "That doesn't sound familiar. Am I supposed to know you?"

"The woman's husband shot and killed my baby brother. I killed him," came the answer.

The old rancher sucked in his breath. This was his son's killer.

"You mean when you two tried to rob the bank and he, as a policeman had to stop you. Now I remember." Tom continued in a loud voice.

"That's right. He killed my brother and I want revenge."

"By killing the policeman's wife? It makes no sense."

"I swore on my brother's grave I'll kill them all."

The man was insane – Tom concluded. It was one thing to take part in a robbery gone wrong and another to plan the murder of a whole family. But then he did kill the policeman. He was a murderer.

"Tell the woman to come forward. I told her not to talk to anybody and she didn't listen. This alone makes me mad and less lenient."

How lenient could a murderer be?

"We have a problem, O'Rourke. The woman and her children are not here. In fact, they are not at my ranch any longer."

"You're lying. I saw them myself."

"Not since two days ago, you didn't."

A pause followed. Then the voice asked, "Did you bring the ring and the bolo tie as I instructed?"

A crow flew above their heads and a shot sounded. O'Rourke was a good shot. The crow fell nearby.

"The bolo tie belongs to John Longlegs. He lost it at the Christmas pageant, in the crowd at the Auditorium. He got it back now, and it is rightfully his."

"No, no. It was magic and it's not right to go to him," the voice behind the rocks wailed.

Tom started to lose patience. "Sure it's right. It was made by his grandfather."

"What about the ring? Did you bring it?"

"What ring?"

"When my brother was shot by the policeman, he had a valuable ring on his finger. When he lay in the funeral parlor, he didn't have it anymore. The police must have taken it and given to the widow."

Ah, another token stolen from someone else. The man was completely insane.

"I know of no ring and I can assure you that the widow doesn't have any other jewelry except her wedding ring." Tom continued. "Your partner has already been arrested…."

"I have no partner. That idiot Williams just got out of prison and thought we were going to ask for ransom and get rich. He had no idea that I planned revenge all along."

"Be reasonable. You can't kill an entire family. Your game is over. The sheriff is waiting to arrest you. Come out peacefully and …," Tom tried to convince him.

Another round of shots was his answer. Tom was thinking of how to lure him out when Donovan jumped up.

"O'Rourke, do you hear me? My name is Donovan. I'm the father of the man you killed."

"Are you crazy? Donovan, get down. He's going to kill you too." Alarmed, Tom tried to pull him down.

A shot sprayed the ground very close to them, making the horses neigh and become agitated. Busy quieting the animals, Tom didn't see that Donovan made himself visible again.

"O'Rourke, come out and fight me like a man," the Texan shouted. "Are you a coward to hide behind the rocks?"

Tom rolled his eyes. "Of course he's a coward. That's what his kind is. It makes him sneaky and lethal. Come down, man." He pulled the older man down just when a shot came so close that one of the horses rose on his hind legs. The Texan fell to the ground. "Donovan, did he hit you?"

The older rancher was dazed. "No, I think the horse pushed me."

"Thank the Lord for that or you'd have been dead. What possessed you to challenge him to a fight?

What do you think this is? A John Wayne movie?"

"I had to make him come out," the Texan muttered.

A tall man came out from behind the rocks and waved his rifle at them. "It's Virgil," Tom said when he saw the Texan grabbing his own gun. He then shouted at Virgil. "Is he dead?"

"No, Boss. I just coshed him over the head with the butt of my rifle."

Virgil tied the hands and feet of the outlaw fast, better than a champion in steer wrestling and dumped him across his saddle. Then he climbed down the narrow path to where they waited.

Donovan studied the small, dirty, man, on Virgil's horse. "He is a puny one," he observed, still miffed at not having the opportunity to confront his son's killer one on one.

"So was Billy the Kid and he was the most lethal killer west of the Mississippi," Tom answered. "You did well, Virgil. Thank you. Take the spare horse and let's mount and run back home. This place is spooky indeed."

"Didn't you say the sheriff is coming?" Donovan asked.

"At the ranch. He's not crazy to ride that far out, unless there are unusual circumstances."

"This is not unusual?" the Texan asked smiling.

"No one's dead, is it? And stop smirking. You Texans have a lot of wild places too, not to mention wild people out there, in the South."

CHAPTER 23

Tom was a man with a mission. He went over the plan in his mind while driving to town. The roads were plowed but a recent flurry had covered the ground with a thin fresh layer of snow. The frost in the early morning hours made the road slippery. But Tom was Wyoming born and bred so a little snow on the road didn't stop him.

Once in Laramie, he parked his truck right in front of TJ Lomax's office.

"Good morning TJ. Did Santa come to you yet?"

TJ raised his eyes from the ancient monitor he still used and waved at Tom to sit down. "It's not Christmas yet. Two days left till then. Besides, I told you I was invited to your house for Christmas. I hope Santa will visit me there, at your place, because he knows better than any GPS where everyone is located."

"You can only hope," Tom grumbled, remembering that there won't be much of a Christmas without Lottie.

"So," TJ leaned back in his chair, crossing his arms over his chest. "…what brings to my humble abode, you, the hero who caught the killer of Wyatt Donovan, our bravest policeman?"

"How did you find this out?" Tom asked surprised the news traveled so fast.

"A private investigator should know what is going on in his town. But this was simple really. Holly, you know Holly Prescott married to Dan who has the auto shop on 3rd and Pine – well Holly, who is secretary at the high school heard from her cousin Trish, who works for the vet, and is niece to Rachael, whose husband is a UPS driver. Very useful to talk to these UPS drivers. They know everything going on in town. So, the driver made a delivery at the sheriff's office and Rhonda, the dispatcher there told him, in strict confidence naturally, that you caught the killer on your ranch."

"Naturally," Tom echoed, feeling his brain expanding to amass all this information. "And from which one of them did you find out?"

"Why, from none of them. Dear Agnes told me."

"Who's dear Agnes?"

TJ looked at him with exasperation. "Miss Proffitt, of course. That's her name, Agnes Proffitt. You kids would know this if you stopped calling her Terror Proffitt."

"She was a terror when I was in high school. Maybe she mellowed over the years," Tom said skeptical. "And she told you?"

"Yes, she did. All in strict confidence, although by then the entire the town had found out."

"Right. It's good to know we have such great and fast communication in town."

"You know what they say, move to a larger town if you want more privacy. It seems the more crowded people are and step on each other's toes, the less they communicate and the less they know about each other. Now, enough talk, what brings you here?"

"Business. I came here on a very serious business matter. You are the best private investigator in town."

"Well. One of the few," TJ added modestly.

"I want to hire you to find me a missing person.

I'll pay you as much as you ask, but it needs to be very fast. In fact, as soon as possible. Definitely before Christmas."

"A missing person. Are you talking about Lottie?"

"Of course, I'm talking about Lottie. And considering how the communication works in this town, I bet you already know where she is. If not, then you can find out easily."

"Maybe she doesn't want to be found or she left town."

Tom shook his head. "No, she didn't leave and she wants to be found. And this is not how it works. I'm paying you to find her."

"Yes, then I need more data."

"About Lottie?"

"I know all I need to know about Lottie. Start by telling me why you want to find her."

"Are you kidding? Because life is unbearable without her. The kitchen is cold. No more radio and Christmas songs. My men are mopping about the place, without anymore whistling or humming, and they look at me accusingly like it is my fault that she left. They keep strict rations of the few remaining cookies baked by Lottie. We wake up hungry and go to bed the same and that is when we stop Brianna from burning another meal. No more vanilla smell or meat roasting in the kitchen, only smoke."

"Man, you could hire a cook, if it's so bad," TJ observed.

"No cook would make such delicious treats for each one of us. Then, the house is again a mess, laundry all mixed together, when it's done. I can never find two socks of a kind. Angel wants a red woolen scarf because he claims Lottie had promised to knit it for him. Virgil said he can't find muffins with almond and poppyseeds like Lottie's anywhere in town."

"What else?"

"On top of it all, I have an old codger in my house, who is set to stay until he sees Lottie and the boys and can't be budged. He's a know-it-all, who sticks his nose into everything. He's more curious than Virgil, if such a thing were possible. Worst of all, he pesters me from morning till night giving me advice on how to manage my ranch. He has an opinion about every little thing and imparts it freely. I've run this ranch alone for years and I'm too set in my ways to accept another's rule."

"What old codger?" TJ asked confused.

"Her father-in-law, that old codger."

"I thought your father passed away a long time ago."

"Of course he did. He was smoking like a furnace. I'm talking about Wyatt Donovan Sr. double Sr. or whatever his name is."

"Oh, you mean the policeman's father came to your house?"

"Yes, he did. Frankly, he's not a bad guy and I wouldn't mind having him around if he were not so interfering. I like to make my own decisions. So, between no-meals in the kitchen and the mismatched laundry, the house is in chaos."

"A housekeeper, you need a good housekeeper,"

TJ said trying to be helpful.

"Will you listen? I don't need a housekeeper. I need Lottie's sweet smile every morning and her singing carols during the day and yes, I need her to organize my whole house and life. I'm lost without her."

TJ nodded approvingly. "Go on. You're on the right path."

"What? I'm not good with words. I need her in my life and I need to feel her velvety skin near me at night."

TJ snapped his mouth shut. Then he said dryly, "Okay, maybe I don't need so much information after all."

But Tom was on a roll. "Because it was a stupid misunderstanding and I love her and can't imagine life without her."

"Is it true?" came a soft voice from the top of the stairs where TJ's private quarters were.

Tom blinked afraid the vision would vanish. Lottie was more beautiful than in his dreams, with her curly honey blond hair and soft hazel eyes, looking at him warily, but with a flicker of hope at the same time, his brave Lottie ready to accept him with all his many faults.

"Yes, of course it's true," he agreed readily, although he had forgotten what was supposed to be true. In fact, Tom found himself tongue-tied and his mind blank. The plan. He had a plan. "Wait here, Lottie. Promise you'll wait here and not go away."

Not understanding what he wanted, Lottie nodded reluctantly. "I promise." And watched amazed as Tom flew out the door.

He returned almost instantly, carrying a pot with a scraggly plant and an old book. He raised his eyes to her. "'Shall I compare thee to a summer's day? Thou art more lovely and more... more...' Wait, I had it here," he said flipping the old pages. "...'temperate...Thou art more lovely and more temperate.' I'm not sure what it means. It sounds strange and not very English, but he must be correct because he was one of the greatest poets."

Lottie sat on the top step and looked at him

crying and laughing at the same time.

"Wait. I know it all, I swear. I repeated it over and over." Only right now his mind was blank and he couldn't remember much. "It's supposed to be one of the best love poems ever written," he finished lamely. "Lottie, don't cry. Here, flowers for you." And he handed her the potted plant. "The flower shop only had poinsettia this time of year, but you already filled my house with them and I wanted some flowers especially for you. This is a Christmas cactus. It had some buds, but I carried it in my truck for two days and I think it lost the buds. The florist assured me it will bloom in December. I wanted red roses, but they had to be special ordered this time of year and they'll arrive in ten days."

"Oh, Tom," Lottie wailed and the next second, she launch herself downstairs in his arms.

"What do you know? The Christmas cactus worked," Tom said, burying his face in her soft curls. "And I had so many doubts about it."

"No, no. It is beautiful and it will bloom," Lottie assured him, wiping her tears.

"Good, then we can go home."

"Wait," TJ stopped him. "Haven't you forgotten something, Tom?"

Tom searched his brain, but didn't come up with anything. The list. He searched his pockets. Ah, yes. He gave Lottie a small velvety box. "I thought that you need a box where to keep your old wedding ring. Place it on your nightstand and it will not get lost."

Lottie opened the box and inside was a simple ring with a diamond winking at her.

"Marry me, Lottie."

"Yes, yes, yes," she cried and hugged and kissed him.

They went to pick up the children from Tristan and Eleanor's house. The day of the Old Man's birthday party, Ellie had found Lottie and the boys wandering on the road and had given them shelter at their house. Tom wanted to tell Ellie what he thought of women interfering where it was not their business, considering the agony she'd put him through. Unfortunately, it was not wise to quarrel with the newly appointed judge, so he only told Tristan that he'd expected more male loyalty from him. Tristan smiled, but it was obvious his loyalty was to his wife.

The boys jumped all over Tom like eager little puppies, asking what was new at the ranch. Was Angel still coughing and did Virgil find his old bridle?

"I'm not sure," Tom answered, "but there is someone waiting for you at the ranch."

"Santa," Billy cried. "Santa came earlier at the ranch. I told you Mama, he's not going to find us in a strange place."

"No, it's not Santa. It's not Christmas yet," Tom explained patiently.

"Then who is it?" Wyatt asked, although half their curiosity was gone, now that they knew it was not Santa and no surprise gifts yet.

"It's your grandfather, who has come all the way from Texas to meet you."

"We don't have a grandfather."

Just then Lottie said, "I don't know, Tom. Wyatt

was adamant not to let the boys be raised by his family."

"And they are going to be raised here, at the ranch, by us. I don't know what happened to estrange Wyatt from his family, but I think the old man is a decent guy. It's your decision, Lottie, of course. Just give him a chance and hear him out."

CHAPTER 24

The boys stopped in the middle of the room, looking warily at the stranger sitting on the couch. Tiger was more forward and came wagging his tail to sniff the man's hand. The old man patted him on the head and scratched behind his floppy ears. Satisfied, the little dog went to play with one of the ornaments hanging on a lower branch of the Christmas tree.

"Are you our Grandfather?" Billy asked.

The man nodded. "Yes, I'm Sam Wyatt Donovan from Texas."

"We never had a grandfather before," Billy said.

"You did. You had me, but I never visited before."

"How come?" Billy continued asking with curiosity.

Wyatt took his hand and pulled him closer. "Did you come to take us with you, mister? Because I warn you that we aren't going. We're staying right here with Mama and Tom." He looked at his brother who bobbed his head up and down in agreement.

"And with Virgil and Hank and Angel. And Tiger and Polly."

"Who's Polly?" Donovan asked with interest.

"The baby goat," Billy explained.

"I see you have a big family here."

Billy came closer, curious like a small child, while Wyatt was more cautious. "Can we call you Grandpa?" He climbed on the couch near Donovan.

"I'd be honored to be called Grandpa," he answered solemnly.

"Just so you understand we are not going with you to Texas," Wyatt emphasized.

Chris, followed by Brianna came in. "Man, it smells divinely in the kitchen and it's not Brianna's burnt meal," he said laughing. Brianna swatted him playfully on the back. "Hey cowboys, I bet you forgot how to ride a horse since you've been away."

"Nah, Tristan had a lot of animals and Zach rides every day. Except that his place is not as big as this," Wyatt observed. He looked at Donovan defiantly, so similar with his father at the same age that Donovan sucked in his breath. Only what little Wyatt said was very different than the memories of his father. "We are going to be cowboys when we grow up, and we'll ride all day like Tom," he said daring Donovan to contradict him.

"That's good. Very good. I'm a rancher myself."

Chris looked from one to the other trying to read their lips. "Well, shall we put it to the test? Are you coming with me to ride?"

The boys jumped in delight and went to take their coats.

"May I come too?" Donovan asked.

"Of course."

Lottie came in the kitchen door. "A moment, Mr. Donovan. Could you come in the kitchen, please? I'm baking cookies and I have to watch them."

"What? Not the famous cupcakes?" he said joking, taking a seat at the large country table.

"I baked those early in the morning." Lottie opened a cupboard and took out a platter she placed on the table. "Please, help yourself."

Donovan picked a chocolate one and took a bite. When the sweet taste filled his mouth, his eyes closed with pleasure.

Lottie looked out the window above the sink. Tom held Wyatt in the saddle in front of him and Billy was riding with Chris, patting the neck of the roan mustang. Her boys were growing up fast. "They are good boys," she said.

"Yes, they are. You raised them well," he agreed.

She turned to face him. She hated confrontations, but sometimes they could not be avoided. "If you came to take them from me, then you'll not succeed. I'll fight you."

He sighed. "I'm not going to say that was not my intention, because it was. But these last days, I got to know Tom and from what I've heard and seen, I know you are a good mother." He looked her up and down. "You're not what I expected, but that is irrelevant."

It was not the first time Lottie was looked over and found wanting. And it still hurt. "What did you expect? Did Wyatt tell you about me?"

"Wyatt and I did not talk. Not a word since he left home at eighteen. No. It was this fellow, Tom Gorman who talked about you from morning till night. According to him, you are the perfect embodiment of all virtues. A goddess come to earth. A siren that lures poor mortals like him."

Lottie looked at him open-mouthed. "You're joking."

"Only a little. The guy is completely smitten. He is a good guy and a fine rancher. You'll do well married to him."

"You know he asked me to marry him?"

Donovan picked a vanilla flavored cupcake. "How could I not to know? He talked only about getting you back and marrying you. Heck, I heard more love poems by that British author, Shakespeare, than I did in high school. I could even recite it myself. 'Shall I compare thee…'. "

Lottie took a deep breath. "He wants to adopt the boys. Do you approve?"

"Yes. He told me that, too. You don't need my approval, but how could I not? I like Tom very much and the boys will be raised to love ranching. I couldn't be more pleased. All I ask is that from time to time, in their vacations, bring them to Texas to see the place where their father grew up and the land that one day will be theirs. They need to know their inheritance and I hope they'll love the land as much as I do."

It was not unreasonable. It was true that Wyatt had been adamant the boys have no contact with his family, but Wyatt was not alive to share parenthood with Lottie and she had to make all the decisions herself. Tom liked Donovan and would whole-heartedly agree to visit the ranch in Texas. The boys showed promise to like ranching and Donovan was right, the Texas ranch was their inheritance. What right had Lottie, or even Wyatt, to forbid them the connection? It was not right.

"I agree. We'll come to Texas." Lottie smiled her agreement. How strange life was and how unpredictable. There was only one issue she needed to clarify. "I hope you don't mind, but I have a question. Wyatt and I, we had a very good marriage. We were honest and devoted to each other and to our boys. I couldn't wish for a better husband. However, there was one thing that Wyatt never talked about and the few times when I asked him, he clammed up and never answered. What caused the rift between you two? I know he didn't like ranching at all, but I always wondered if perhaps this was only to antagonize you as rebellious teenagers usually do. He was a decent rider, unlike me. What could have been so bad for him to leave home for good and never talk to his family?"

The older Texas rancher sighed and looked at his work-roughened hands as they rested on the table. "As you said, he claimed he hated the ranch, but I thought it was a passing phase. After all, how could a man not love the land where he was born? When Wyatt was eighteen, and had just graduated from high school, I told him he was not my son. He took his duffel bag and left without a word."

"Was it true?" Lottie asked. People throw words carelessly sometimes, without thinking of the consequences.

"I was Wyatt's father in every way that mattered. I was there when he was born, when he was sick as a child, and I taught him everything I knew and thought important. It was not enough apparently. Everything I had to give was not good enough." He sighed again, the deep emotion threatening to overwhelm him. In a low voice, barely audible, he said, "Biologically, he was not mine. Only Alicia is. I thought it didn't matter, but … in the end, it did."

Oh, poor man. Lottie's generous heart cried for him. "No, it doesn't matter. I'm sure the shock of hearing this was too much for eighteen-year-old Wyatt, but the boys have already accepted you as their grandfather, the only one they have. We'll visit Texas often. It will work, you'll see."

"Thank you," he said, his voice cracking.

EPILOGUE

The wedding of Tom Gorman and Lottie Donovan took place the day after Christmas in the small church on the outskirts of town where they all worshipped. In attendance were family, friends, neighbors, curious people come to see the most famous bachelor in these parts finally getting married. Even some policemen, who considered Lottie one of their own, were present to wish her happiness. The church was packed despite the frigid day outside.

The groom, whose best men were his brother Chris and his man, Virgil, was pacing in front waiting for the ceremony to start. In the front row, the Texan rancher, S. W. Donovan was flanked by his two grandsons, who were twisting their necks looking behind to see their mother come in.

First entered the two matrons-of-honor, blonde, regal, newly appointed Judge Eleanor Maitland and tall, brunette, green-eyed Faith Maitland, both dressed in pale-blue satin dresses.

"Oh man, I swear these two are the most beautiful women I've seen in my life," a cheeky young man from the audience said. He was shushed, but everyone present agreed with him.

And then the organist started to play the wedding march and Lottie entered the church on the arm of TJ Lomax. She wore a deceptively simple, ankle-long dress of off-white velvet, with discreet gold embroidery at the edge. It was flowing beautifully, molding to Lottie's generous curves, emphasizing her shape and making her look somewhat taller.

And when she looked into her groom's eyes, so full of admiration and love, Lottie smiled and all her anxiety disappeared. This day, here, Lottie Donovan, soon-to-be Gorman, felt she was the most beautiful woman on earth. And no one present doubted it. Today she was the belle of the ball.

The wedding celebration continued at the Gorman ranch and as it was customary here, everyone who wanted to come was welcome. Despite the short time for preparations, food appeared on the tables. People rejoiced this opportunity for celebration and merriment in the dreary winter months.

The carpet was rolled in the living and family room and couples were turning around the floor to the sound of well-known country music.

Tom had just twirled his bride one more time making her laugh, when he saw Angel in the doorway, inclining his head, signaling Tom to follow him outside. Tom sighed. He had no peace on his wedding day. Trouble lay ahead. Kissing Lottie briefly he excused himself and followed Angel outside.

Angel passed the barn where a few of the guests had gathered too and went straight to the bunkhouse. Inside, his men were gathered around Virgil, who looked so dejected like his world had ended.

"What's going on here?" Tom asked.

"I'm sorry, Boss. It is your wedding and all, but I think you should be informed right away," Angel said. "Virgil found this tacked to one of the stall doors in the barn."

Without words, Virgil gave Tom a piece of paper. It said:

"Dear Tom, I didn't want to interrupt your wedding celebration. When you read this, I'll be far away. I decided to leave with Joe. It is time for me to find my way in life. I wish you a long happy marriage. Lottie is super.

Love, Brianna"

"She left," Virgil said simply, unable to believe it was true.

Tom read once more the short message. "Who the heck is Joe?"

"Joe Brown, or so he calls himself. From the Maitland ranch," Hank explained.

"The one Virgil fought at the Old Man's birthday bash?"

"Yep, that's the one. Smooth talker with the ladies and dirty fighting with the men. Bad news, all in all."

In what heap of trouble had his little sister jumped? Tom clenched his fist. "I'm going after her.

They can't be far."

"No." The single word reverberated with authority in the bunkhouse. Lottie stood in the door, dressed in all her wedding finery. No one dared to tell her that the bunkhouse was by unspoken rules, off limits to women. It was the place where the men, played poker, drank, undressed, talked dirty, said jokes and generally felt free to act like men.

It seemed Lottie was not aware of these rules or right now she didn't care. She walked toward them. "No, not because today is my wedding day, but because Brianna is a grown woman of almost thirty, free to come and go as she pleases. More than that, she has been restless recently, and torn between loving this ranch and feeling there should be more to life. She needed a change."

"And you think Joe Brown is the needed change?"

"No, of course not. And I don't think she loves him. He is only an excuse, a means to go away. Let her go. She needs to fly or she'll feel stifled." She touched

Virgil gently on the arm. "I'm sorry, Virgil."

"I know, Miss Lottie. Even if she'd stayed, she wouldn't look at the likes of me."

Later, much later that night, with Lottie's soft body nestled in his arms, Tom kissed the sweet delicate skin at her nape and asked in the darkness, "Do you suppose she'll be back?"

"Of course she will. But she needs to discover first what she wants and what makes her happy. She needs to fly."

"You had a lot of flying to do in your life, Lottie."

"Yes, but in the end it brought me to you."

"I'm a lucky man," he said, tightening his hold on his bride.

In the kitchen, on the counter, where a scraggly looking plant had been placed in a nice looking clay pot, at the end of one green stem a bright fuchsia-colored bud unfurled into a beautiful bell-shaped flower.

VIVIAN SINCLAIR

* * *

Keep reading for an excerpt from 'A Visitor For Christmas', book 2 of the *Wyoming Christmas* series:

A Visitor For

Christmas

PROLOGUE

The boy hid in the loft, burrowed deep in the hay. The welts on his back hurt with every move he made. Some were older and not properly healed crisscrossed by the new ones he got today. His stepfather's belt caught him on the fresh wound he got the day before on his left shoulder from the barbed wire.

"Virgil," his mother's voice called.

The boy sank deeper into the hay. His ma was powerless against her husband. She tried once to defend him and it enraged Virgil's stepfather and made the beating worse. Since then she'd never tried again.

"Virgil," she called louder. "He's not here," she reported outside and left closing the barn doors.

Later, much later, after midnight, when no one was around, Virgil made his way down the ladder, tiptoeing carefully. He said good-bye to the horse he'd raised from birth and which was to be sold next day, he ruffled the hair of the barn cat, and patted the two cows in the stalls.

When he was ready to leave, he saw a small bundle near the door. Two clean shirts, a pair of woolen socks, and seventeen wrinkled one-dollar bills. It was all his mother could hide from her husband.

Virgil was grateful for this. It was better than nothing. It was his inheritance, or all he was ever going to get.

Slowly, he stepped outside and made his way into the dark night, leaving behind the Montana ranch that had been the pride of his father and before him of his ancestors. He was twelve years old.

CHAPTER 1

It was that time of year again. The beginning of December. The ranch house was decorated with greenery, lights in all the windows and strings along the edge of the roof. Inside, a majestic fir tree in the bow window of the family room sported all the decorations that had been hidden in the attic for generations. Even the bunkhouse was gifted with a smaller tree and the barn, ornate with multicolored lights, had a huge red bow hung on top of the doors. All the cowboys were walking around whistling and humming merry carols. All, except Virgil.

He was not a Scrooge. Usually, Virgil liked Christmas just fine. This year however, it brought back painful memories of his hopeless, lost love. A year ago at Christmas, Brianna Gorman, his Boss' sister had run away with a no-good cowboy from a neighboring ranch. At first, Virgil didn't believe she just left, abandoning the ranch where she grew up and her family. Oh, he knew she didn't care about him. After all, he was just a poor, simple cowboy, not very handsome and certainly no smooth talker like the oily man she'd left with. She told Virgil many times that he meant nothing to her. But still, he waited, hoping she'd realize the man she chose was not worthy of her. Hoping she'd see she made a mistake and came back.

As the months went by, one after the other, his hope withered, like an unattended flame. Now it was almost extinguished.

In the kitchen, the music sounded at full blast, "Jingle bells, jingle bells…" and in front of the stove, Lottie, the Boss' wife was stirring in a large pot, moving in rhythm with the song. The flavors of garlic and herbs from the beef stew were almost overpowering the vanilla and cinnamon from the many cakes and cookies Lottie was baking continuously this time of year.

The smell alone was so enticing that it could break a man's determination to do what needed to be done. Sighing, Virgil grabbed an almond and poppyseed muffin, his favorite; Lottie baked them especially for him. They were on a platter near the snickerdoodle cookies that Angel, the mountain man, liked so much.

Wrapping another muffin in a napkin, to savor later, Virgil made his way toward the Boss' study. He knocked briefly and entered his Boss' private space, with all-around shelves bending under the load of old, leather bound books, mixed with newer paperbacks and spiral binders of various sizes. Virgil inhaled the familiar smell of leather and cigars smoked years ago by generations of less health-conscious ranchers.

Tom Gorman was frowning at the screen of his computer and absently waved at Virgil to sit down. Finally, he raised his eyes. "Ah, Virgil. Just the man I wanted to talk to." Looking at him, Tom noticed that something was wrong with his man. "What happened? Tell me."

"It's time for me to go, Boss," Virgil said with sadness.

Tom didn't pretend he didn't understand. "Where would you go? Do you have plans?"

Virgil shook his head. "No. I figured I could go south, to a warmer climate, Oklahoma, Texas. Someone will need a cowboy with a strong back."

"Listen, Virgil. You know I appreciate and respect you. Hank is telling me that he wants to retire and I intended to make you foreman. What do you say?"

"Why me? Why not your brother, Chris?"

"Chris is good and hard-working, but he prefers working with horses, being out on the range, not organizing and giving orders."

"True," Virgil agreed. He paused and placed the napkin on the desk. Unwrapping the muffin, he broke it in two and gave Tom half.

Tom accepted the offering, ate his half in two bites. "Good muffin. Are there any of the pink cupcakes left in the kitchen?"

"I think so. Lottie is in a frenzy of cooking. You'd think Christmas is tonight, not in four weeks."

"Yeah," Tom's face softened thinking of his wife. "She is a natural-born nurturer."

"There is no other like her. I'll miss her and her cooking. And the boys." The boys were Lottie's children from the first marriage, now adopted by Tom.

"They adore you. They follow you around like two little puppies," Tom said. "You are practically part of this family, Virgil."

"You don't know how much this means to me, Boss. I've never had a family since my Dad died when I was six. I was just a lone drifter."

The door opened and Lottie came in carrying a plate with two huge roast beef sandwiches and a plate with chocolate chip cookies freshly baked. She placed them on Tom's desk. "You two can't decide the fate of the world without having some sustenance. Here is your lunch." Tom pulled her down in his lap and gave her a fleeting kiss. His eyes promised more for later in the privacy of their room. Laughing Lottie returned to the kitchen.

Seeing the obvious love between the two, made Virgil more determined to leave. "What can I do, Boss? I waited a year hoping Brianna would come to her senses and return. I should have known that she is too stubborn and too proud to admit she made a mistake. Besides, it's pointless. Even if she came home, there is no hope for me. It's not like I changed into Prince Charming over night. I'm still my ugly self."

Virgil was not exactly ugly, although Tom was not an expert in masculine beauty, but his face was rather homely. If you added to that the fact that he wore his heart on a sleeve and his love for Brianna was not a secret, then it was no wonder that Brianna didn't take him seriously and was annoyed by his attention.

Women were a mystery for Tom and he thanked his lucky stars that he had found such a treasure of a wife like Lottie. Tom didn't understand why his sister could not appreciate Virgil who was hard-working and honest, not to mention tall and well-built. "Listen, there is something that you don't know. When Brianna was eighteen she fell hard for a handsome, but lazy cowboy, who had been hired for the summer at our ranch."

"Yes, I know," Virgil replied.

"I bet you do. The Gorman siblings are famous for falling in love with the wrong people. It's common knowledge in these parts."

"Not really. The cowboys talk at the bunkhouse

of this and that."

Tom laughed. "Worse than gossiping old women. I know. Back to our story. This cowboy dared come to my old man to tell him that he was willing to go away and leave Brianna behind, for a price. Frankly, I think he intended to do this anyhow, but he figured the old man was gullible enough to pay. He didn't know my old man very well. Dear Dad not only didn't pay, but also chased him away with his whip, a trait he got from his friend and neighbor, Maitland. To talk and argue with people while cracking his whip on the side."

When Virgil looked at him horrified, Tom explained, "No, he didn't use it on people. It was used only to strengthen his arguments. It was all for show. Although, I wondered if on that particular occasion, he was not tempted to flog the scoundrel. Anyhow, this reinforced his opinion that Brianna is not able to take care of herself and that the land needed protected from such an unfortunate situation."

"Brianna is perfectly able to take care of herself," Virgil argued on behalf of the woman he loved.

"You'd think so, but look what happened again. Another rogue came along and Brianna fell for him. After the old man died, the will was read by Dad's lawyer. Hearing that she got no part of the land, only a large sum of money and with Dad's message that he hoped this will help her find a worthy husband, Brie left in a huff. So she didn't hear another small proviso our Dad wrote in his will. Even the money willed to Brianna cannot be used unless I approve it."

"This is really insulting to Brianna."

Tom nodded. "I thought so too, at the time. Now, I'm not so sure. You see, it's true that I had no communication with Brianna since she left a year ago. But in the spring, she contacted the lawyer to withdraw her money."

"All of it?"

"Yep, all of it. And trust me, it was quite a lot of money. Per the proviso in the will, the lawyer asked me what to do. I agreed to her demand only if she came home to talk to me. I am her brother after all and she must know I care about her."

"Still it would be humiliating to return home asking for the money that is hers," Virgil observed, ever so loyal to Brianna.

"Just as well she didn't come. In autumn, she tried to have this proviso annulled arguing that she was a thirty-year-old woman and able to make decisions on her own. No luck here as the law is very clear – a man can write in his will whatever he wants. Unless he is not sound of mind, his will is valid."

"Do you know anything else about her?" Virgil asked.

"I asked TJ Lomax, the private investigator from Laramie, to keep tabs on her. Last I heard, she was in Denver working in a restaurant."

"I hope not cooking." Brianna was famous for her burnt meals, before Lottie had moved in to take over the kitchen.

"No, not cooking or they would have fired her immediately. She was hostess or waitress or something like that. My point is, I know my sister, she needs to sit on a horse and ride free on the range, not to be cooped up all day in a smelly restaurant. I'm sure whatever love there was between her and that cowboy, has since vanished. It always does in such cases when there is no money. And city life is not for Brianna. She'll be back soon, mark my word. If you would only wait a few more months…"

Virgil thought about it. It was tempting, oh, so tempting. But in the end, there was no happy ending for him. "No, even if Brianna returns home, it doesn't mean she is in love with me. Let's face it. I'm not her ideal of a perfect man."

"No man is perfect, Virgil. What you have to do is to ask Lottie from time to time what would impress my crazy sister. She'll give you good advice. Otherwise, who knows what women consider perfect?"

Virgil shook his head. "Even if she were to look at me more favorably, she will never love me. I'd be miserable loving her as I do and she - she'd feel trapped with a man who is not her first choice. Do you understand this, Tom?"

Of course, Tom understood. He, himself had been

most of his adult life in love with a beautiful woman who was his girlfriend because she found no one better, but who considered him dull and boring. Falling in love with Lottie had been like freeing himself from invisible chains. Could he deny Virgil the same chance? "Tell you what, it's Christmastime. No one should spend it alone. Stay with us until January and then decide what you want to do. Besides, Lottie wouldn't allow you to leave before spending Christmas with us. She is preparing a huge celebration, gifts for everybody, singing carols, a lot of food and fun time."

Taking the last cookie from the plate, Virgil nodded. "Very well. And thank you for everything."

To find out about new releases and about other books written by Vivian Sinclair visit her website at VivianSinclairBooks.com or follow her on the Author page at Amazon or on GoodReads.com

Virginia Lovers Trilogy - contemporary romance:

    Book 1 – Alexandra's Garden

    Book 2 – Ariel's Summer Vacation

    Book 3 – Lulu's Christmas Wish

A Guest At The Ranch – western contemporary romance

Maitland Legacy, A Family Saga Trilogy - western contemporary romances

    Book 1, Lost In Wyoming – Lance's story

    Book 2, Moon Over Laramie – Tristan's story

    Book 3, Christmas In Cheyenne – Raul's story

Wyoming Christmas Trilogy – western contemporary romances

    Book 1 – Footprints In The Snow – Tom's story

A VISITOR FOR CHRISTMAS

Book 2 – A Visitor For Christmas – Brianna's story

Book 3 – Trapped On The Mountain – Chris' story

Seattle Rain series - women's fiction novels

Book 1 - A Walk In The Rain

Book 2 – Rain, Again!

Book 3 – After The Rain

Storm In A Glass Of Water, a small town story

Made in the USA
San Bernardino, CA
09 December 2016